A MORE PERFECT LOVE

KATE FOREST

A MORE PERFECT LOVE

Ruby Basset Publishing, publisher

For B and L

L'dor v'dor

ACKNOWLEDGEMENTS

Since leaving my day jobs, I thought I would be isolated as a writer. Turns out I spend even more time collaborating with others than in any other job. The many eyes that have read and reread this story: My fabulous critique team of Veronica Forand, Susan Scott Shelley, Lauren Strauss, Maria Imbalzano, and Kate Lutter. A special thank you to Stephen M. Silverman, who actually agreed to talk with me on the phone about the history of the Catskills. Check out his book, The Catskills, for a rich and surprising history.

My personal support team: The Mah Jongg Moms. My parents, who never sit at the first table they're shown at a restaurant. The real writer of the family, Andrea Pyros. My kids, to whom I have dedicated this book. They are the beneficiaries of a diversity of legacies. And the hero of my own romance story. Smooches to you, dear husband.

Chapter 1

CATHY

Even with Pine Breeze Resort restored to its former paradise, my jitters weren't eased. When New York City summer temperatures became unbearable, anyone who could escape escaped to the Catskills. Pine Breeze was *the* place to escape. But in the past few years, it had suffered from a lack of men, food, and happy families. Finally, with the return of "our boys" from the Pacific theater, the Catskills were restored.

"Cathy, your father is ready. Stop daydreaming." Mom's trousers were rolled up so she wouldn't get any sand on the cuffs and her hair was covered in a scarf to keep her 'do from being wrecked by the wind.

"Coming." This was my chance. Whatever family outing we were headed to would be the stage for my announcement.

My daydreaming mind had been estimating the number of chairs on the beach and calculating the density of trees between the lake and the road. My daydreaming mind had graduated top of my class from Vassar and landed me an actuarial job at the biggest insurance company in Philadelphia. With only four weeks left until I was expected to report, I had to say something to my family soon.

"When we get back, we're going to meet the others for

a swim." Marilyn, my engaged-to-be-married-to-the-perfect-boy older sister, seemed just as restored as the resort, as if the past few years of war had never happened.

"It's too cold for swimming." I trailed behind her, meandering through the lines of chairs that packed the "shore" of Liberty Lake.

She ignored me. "Try not to go off on one of your mathematics lectures. This is the summer you should find a husband."

"I don't lecture." And I didn't want a husband. "Where are we going anyway?"

Mom smiled and shook her head. "My silly girl who never pays attention. I explained at breakfast that Daddy wants to spend some time with Mr. Bergen."

Submerging myself in the frigid water was looking more appealing. I didn't want Mr. Bergen to be there when I revealed my plans. Yes, he was Daddy's best friend as well as the resort owner, but he also liked to butt his nose into everyone else's business. Daddy was likely to bristle at the idea of my moving to a new city, but when he was at Pine Breeze, he was amenable to almost anything. It was here, three years ago, that I convinced him that majoring in mathematics wasn't a waste of time for a girl. I hoped for a repeat performance of my persuasive skills.

Sure enough, Daddy, Marilyn's fiancé David, and Mr. Bergen waited for us at the beachside entrance to the main building of the resort.

"There's our graduate. What do you think, Bergen? Could you have ever guessed our Cathy would take college by storm?" Daddy pulled me into an embrace and kissed the top of my head.

"She's not the little girl who used to pilfer cookies from the kitchen and take them along with a book up in the tree like a squirrel." Mr. Bergen hugged me. "You have a lot to celebrate, Gold. One daughter engaged, another graduated. Your youngest still in school?"

"For the time being. Beth is threatening to drop out and run to Palestine if I don't keep an eye on her. Boarding school is the best place for her. Got her all safe and sound."

"It's called Israel now, Daddy," I corrected him, although he ignored the comment and placed his focus on Mom.

"She comes home in a week and will join us then." Mom had ached when Beth had gone away to school. We three were all she had. When Beth had jumped at the chance to get out of the house, Mom caved. She wouldn't keep any of her daughters from pursuing their dreams.

"You're a very lucky man." Mr. Bergen's voice faltered. No one mentioned his elder son Lawrence, whose body couldn't even be returned to him. Left with only his younger son, who came home after two weeks in basic training with a broken toe that healed incorrectly, Mr. Bergen's grief would most likely stay with him forever. The loss of the son he'd counted on to inherit the business showed in his half smile instead of the natural warmth I remembered.

He cleared his throat. "Well, folks, I promised you a tour of our new resort. I want you to be the first to see how it's coming along. This way to the van."

"What new resort?" I asked Mom as we filed through the beach access door and into the resort lobby.

She sighed. "I explained it this morning. Mr. Bergen is building a new place on the next lake over. Daddy invested some money in it."

The main dining room was vacant except for the sparse crew setting up for dinner, which would be served by harried waiters unceremoniously shoving plates of roasted chicken under our faces. The ballroom at the other end bustled with a cleaning staff so the floor would be ready for evening dancing, where girls would flaunt dresses with increasingly high hemlines, in desperate attempts to catch the attention of boys who were recently soldiers. And no one would be interested in anything interesting. But I did like dancing, just not all the promises that went along with the closeness.

As we neared the grand front entrance, Mr. Bergen stopped and chatted with a young man wearing a plain black suit, out of place for the casual wear of the resort.

"Gold family, let me introduce Thomas Cullen, my most trusted manager."

"Pleased to make your acquaintances." Instead of shaking hands, Mr. Cullen kept them clasped behind his back and offered us a brief bow.

I stifled a laugh at this old-fashioned gesture. But what really bubbled inside of me was the way his flame-red hair fell across his brow and made his piercing blue eyes seem even bluer. I had always been a Humphrey Bogart kind of girl, going for the dark, handsome types. But his eyes had me changing my mind.

Marilyn's elbow contacted with my side to break me from staring.

"Thomas came here as a building engineer to maintain our aging boiler and electricity," Mr. Bergen said. "If you've got working lights in your room, it's because of Thomas."

"Well, thank you, Thomas," Mom said. "I certainly wouldn't enjoy my vacation if I couldn't read before bed at night."

"Always reading, always doing her puzzles. She never lets her mind rest." Dad took Mom's arm in his and beamed with the honor of having a brilliant wife.

"Are you all enjoying your stay?" Thomas Cullen's words were laced with a slight Irish accent, but his tenor voice was strong. The flash of white teeth in his sun-darkened face sent flutters to my belly.

"Cathy complains about the lake being too cold. She's such a fuddy-duddy, and prefers a game of chess to volleyball." Marilyn was never one to pass up an opportunity to point out my flaws.

"Well, Miss Gold, I'm afraid I can do nothing about the water temperature in the lake. God has plans for that. But I hope there's no lack of amusements for you."

I couldn't keep the laugh down. His chivalrous tone should have been too formal to be warm, but my insides rippled like the lake. "I find amusements enough, Mr. Cullen. My friends make sure of that. They insist I join them to cut a rug tonight."

"I'm sure you'll have your choice of partners." Mr. Cullen winked and conferred over some details with Mr.

Bergen before he turned his attention to the registration desk.

The rest of us exited through the front and onto the vast green that led to the circular drive.

"Why can't you flirt like that with Will Hartman?" Marilyn muttered.

"I wasn't flirting." I didn't mean to flirt, but he was so arrestingly handsome. I most definitely was changing my mind about blue eyes. His maturity fit him, not like Will and the others just trying on their manly attitudes. Mr. Cullen spiked my curiosity. Will didn't spike anything for me.

Under the portico, Mr. Bergen's driver waited at his Packard. We all scooted in and, with me practically on Mom's lap, we lurched onto the dirt road that led away from the resort.

"This road will be paved over before the winter comes," Mr. Bergen explained from the front seat, where Daddy was sandwiched between him and the driver. "Your jaw will drop open when you see this location. Boy, your jaw will drop."

After a few minutes of jostling, the car crested a hill, and my jaw did indeed drop.

Perfect woods surrounded a pristine lake, smaller than the one at Pine Breeze. A small rise to one side was being cleared by men and machines.

"Get out here. You'll want to see it as we walk." Mr. Bergen directed his driver to go on ahead and meet us at the work site. "Doesn't the air feel even cleaner here?"

I wasn't sure if the air felt cleaner, but the solitude,

despite the noise from the workmen, brought welcome relief from the constant commotion of the bustling resort we were used to.

"Bergen, you have picked a prime spot. I knew going in with you was no mistake."

"Come and see the Belvedere." Mr. Bergen motioned for us to follow.

We picked our way along the ridge and down to the site.

"Now, see over there, no more bungalows. Actual cottages. And no enormous dining hall filled with tasteless noise. We're having intimate, sophisticated restaurants, three of them. You'll be able to choose the type of meal you want. Except at breakfast, that will be served buffet style. Available whenever you want between seven and ten."

Following him into the frame of a large structure, we watched Mr. Bergen turn in a circle with his arms outstretched. "And this is our theater. It will have dancing, an orchestra, and performers. But none of those Lower East Side *tummlers* we have now. High-class acts. Singers who sound like birds, actors performing Shakespeare. I tell you, Gold, the next thing in resorts is high end. All those GIs coming home? They have money in their pockets, and they'll be flooding Pine Breeze, and I'll welcome them. But this, this place will be for the likes of you and me. A classy place for our people."

Daddy nodded and turned in the same circle.

"Thomas Cullen is going to be manager here to get things going. Nothing like a strict Irishman to keep the troops in line."

I tried to picture the suave Mr. Cullen barking orders. Maybe he was stern with the help and all flash for the guests. He seemed like a puzzle waiting to be solved.

"I like Pine Breeze," Mom said.

"Mom, it was fun when we were kids. But now, something more refined would be a welcome change," Marilyn said, squeezing David's arm.

"I like that it's quiet," I added.

"Yes, your daughters understand. Quiet, refined." Mr. Bergen's face shone with joy I hadn't seen in him for a long time.

I rolled my eyes. "Not sure how refined the Catskills can get. But peaceful is nice."

My words were lost on Daddy and Mr. Bergen as they went into deeper discussions.

"Are you having a good time so far?" Mom pulled me aside and rested a hand on my shoulder.

"I guess. Maybe I'm too old for the resort now. It's the same every year."

"I hope twenty-one isn't too old. What does that make me?" She squeezed my arm and pecked my cheek. "We're so proud of you. You know that, right? First in your class."

"Yes, but I have some ideas about what my plan should be." I dug my fingernails into my palms to keep from blurting out my news.

"Will Hartman has a plan." Mom smiled.

"Not one I want to go along with." I took in the scenery. "It's beautiful here. I could stay here forever without having a plan."

"That's silly. Who stays in the Catskills forever?"

The car waited for us at the end of the construction site. Mom's sling-backs were hopelessly muddy, and another jarring ride back awaited us. But the stunning landscape made the time with Mr. Bergen worth the trip.

Already, Mom mentioned meeting her friends for bridge and Marilyn said she was going off to play tennis when we returned. My family was about to scatter again. Crammed together in the car was the only time I was going to get them in one place. And I had practically burst with the news twice in the last hour. Maybe having Mr. Bergen there would be to my benefit. Daddy wouldn't lose his cool in front of his friend. The next time we'd all be together was in the dining hall—hardly the quiet place I needed.

The bumpy ride back to Pine Breeze wasn't ideal, but the words exploded out.

"I have something big to tell you all." I took a deep breath as Daddy craned his neck from the front seat.

"We can wait to hear it when we get back." Mom's strained voice was in my ear since we were pressed together.

"I can't wait."

"Cathy." Daddy's scolding tone gave me pause. His warning seemed out of place. It wasn't like we weren't all family. Mr. Bergen was more of an uncle to me than Mom's brother.

"Let Cathy talk," Marilyn said. "I'm dying to know what's had her all twisted up today."

My sister might be the older, more obedient one. But

she knew me better than anyone, and her encouragement spurred me on.

"I'm moving to Philadelphia. I'm going to be an actuary." My heart flickered in my chest, and I tried to sit up straighter under Mom.

Mr. Bergen kept his eyes fixed out the side window. Daddy slowly turned his head forward again and the muscle in his jaw pulsed.

"Well." Marilyn's smile was a small, sad expression of pity. She patted my arm and whispered, "Wowee, did you think Daddy would go for that? Didn't you learn anything at that college?"

"We should be back any minute," Mom said as if we were returning from a shopping trip.

"Daddy?" My brain went fuzzy. I hadn't expected a full-hearted *mazel tov*, but I wanted some reaction.

"Wait, Cathy," was all he would say.

The silence hammered my ears more than the construction machines.

I had missed something down the line. They were neither surprised, nor excited, nor angry.

The car rolled into the driveway of the main entrance. Mr. Bergen opened the door before the wheels stopped. Marilyn and David scurried out, too.

I stayed in my seat. My gut told me that nothing good awaited me outside that Packard.

Mom scooted out, gave the slightest nod, and turned to go inside.

Daddy stood in the driveway and held a hand out to

me. I took it, but the comforting protection it usually offered wasn't there.

He directed me toward the path that went around the perimeter of the property. It wasn't used much since the quickest way to the lake, the tennis courts, and anything else was a straight line.

I stopped in my tracks, only a few yards from where we started. "I know what you're going to say. But I've checked everything out. I have a safe place to live and I'll be making enough—"

"Do you know what it's like to find out that your daughter has taken a job in a different city without letting you know?" He took his arm away from mine. "I had to find out from Matthew Ginsberg, the New York representative for that company. He also happens to be a member of the country club."

"I'm so sorry, Daddy. I wanted to tell you I was looking for work, but I wanted to do it all on my own. I didn't want you to pull strings with your friends." I touched his shoulder. "I didn't mean to embarrass you."

He looked past me at the crowds leaving the beach as the sun was dipping at the water's edge. "Sweetheart, I love you and I need to protect you, even if that's from yourself and your unconventional ideas."

A flutter of excitement still lingered in my chest. "I've got it all planned out. I've found a boardinghouse where I can join some other girls—"

Daddy held up a hand. "You will not. You'll live at home and you can work for me as a secretary in my office until you get married."

"What did you think I would do with a degree in mathematics? I have a job. A good job." My throat was as dry as dust, but my eyes stung with tears. The man who'd always cheered me on no longer supported me.

"No, Cathy, you don't. I asked Matthew to put me in touch with the Philadelphia office and I explained that my naïve daughter wouldn't be living on her own in a strange city."

"You got me fired?" My head pounded. I knew my voice was louder than what he wanted, but I didn't care.

"You can't get fired if you never worked there. You'll find a letter from them when we get home. I'm sorry. But I know what it's like to live in those kinds of places. I know what it's like to be on your own in a big city. It's not safe, and it's certainly not safe for a young, innocent Jewish girl."

"You've always said education is important for us. Why is anything different now?"

"It is important. And I can't be more proud of what you've achieved. But you have a responsibility to your people. To your family. After what happened. Haven't you been saying you want to do your part? The Jewish population needs mothers. Honor the sacrifice your grandparents made by continuing the family."

Daddy might have said more, but I didn't hear it. Anguish and despair flooded my senses. Daddy's stricken face reflected the cry I let loose. I turned and ran. I didn't care who saw me. I didn't care what the gossip would be at dinner that night.

I had one dream. One goal. A job and independence. Daddy had denied me any chance to help my country. I had watched my classmates serve, while I waited and studied. Doing well in school was the only way I could prevent anyone from keeping me from making my own decisions. Reaching my goals should have been easy for someone who graduated summa cum laude.

Dashing through the lobby and out the other side of the main building toward the bungalows, I heard someone call my name. I didn't stop. I flew down the steps and the path. Sobs and gulps of air rocked my body. I was dizzy when I reached the bungalow I shared with Marilyn. Ignoring her question, I flung myself into the bathroom and locked the door, then sat on the floor, waiting for the sobs to end. If they never ended, that would be fine with me.

***

THOMAS

I watched Bergen's car drive away with the Gold family a moment longer than I should have. If there was one thing this job didn't afford, it was a spare moment.

Using the service entrance, I wound my way to the dairy kitchen. If my dear departed *athair* ever thought I would end up serving kosher meals, he might never have taken my pregnant mother on that dangerous Atlantic crossing. As it was, I was born on American soil. Almost literally, as I think there was no floor in the first factory-owned shack we lived in.

"My sweet Ethel, we will be needing those cakes for

dessert tonight. You're starting to give me a wee bit o' nerves that you're only mixing the batter now." I dialed up all my charms for the elderly baker. She might move slowly, but her confections disappeared fast.

"Don't sweet-talk me, Mr. Cullen. You can't rush cakes."

Oh, how I wished I could rush everything. But with her talent with pastries, I'd learned to have patience with Ethel Nussbaum. Besides her talent, she'd lost both her young sons in battle, and her husband long before. It was our duty to make sure she had work until she could no longer beat an egg.

I made my late-afternoon rounds. Which, when completed, meant it would be time to change into my tux and do my pre-dinner rounds, dinner supervision, post-dinner rounds, and entertainment supervision, give orders to the late cleanup crew, fall into bed at two in the morning. Awake at five and start the fun again.

I wouldn't complain for an instant. Because there aren't many people who would hire a man without an education and a few important fingers. Mr. Bergen had been good to me since I came looking for work from over the hill. The Irish Catskills on the north side of the mountains were considerably less impressive than the Jewish side. Our pleasures were simple and no one much cared about a fancy orchestra. A few men with a fiddle and you had yourself a clogging party.

"Mail for you, Mr. Cullen." The inefficient and curt bellhop bellowed as he ran, and thrusted a pile of letters at me.

"Thanks, Sam." I flipped through them, realizing that Sam would never advance far if he couldn't learn a little more tact. Then again, he might have had dreams beyond the Catskills. Hard for me to understand why anyone would want to live anywhere else. But people did.

The last letter in the stack was written in the neat hand of my mother's neighbor. There was always the chance Ma had passed on, but most often a letter from Mrs. Clatchy was just Ma's thoughts transcribed. Handwriting never came easy to her.

I tucked that one into my pocket. Saving it for the small minutes I could savor the news of my younger sister earning top marks at the school she could afford because of my labors. By American standards, it wasn't expensive to send a child to a good school in Dublin. But it was near impossible by Irish standards. And with every kind of shortage over there, I was more than grateful Ma could keep Maggie in school.

There wasn't much choice anyway after Da died. Despite the war, Ireland was the only place they could be. My American dollars could go further in Ireland. And with every second cent of my wage, they lived comfortably without Maggie having to go into drudgery factory work. Every additional cent went toward building my dream.

"Mr. Cullen, sir." A young dishwasher approached.

"Yes, Billy?"

"I was hoping to have tonight off. My family is staying at the *cuchulains* down the road. Ma's so thrilled to finally have a kitchen to herself in the cabin."

"We're packed tonight, son. Everyone is going to want to eat dinner."

His crestfallen face twisted me.

"Fine, but you owe me a shift." I wagged a finger on my left hand at him. Always careful to keep my right hand hidden when possible. No one wanted to see deformity at a resort.

"Thanks, Mr. C." He scampered off, and I knew I'd be washing dishes in my tux tonight.

I debated where my attention should go next when I spotted someone who didn't belong in the main lobby.

Garrett Laron, with all the confidence that comes from being a one-time thief, lit a cigarette in the corner and took stock of the room. His slightly worn but fashionable herringbone was probably his best suit, but he had come a long way from petty robbery into almost legitimate work as a land broker, and the change shone not just in his wardrobe, but in his newly cleansed soul. Even if his eyes did wander to the necklaces of the women who passed by.

"Don't be lifting any wallets in my place." I clasped his shoulder.

"Thomas, the easy life suits you. You fill out those clothes like someone getting three hot meals a day."

"I work here, I eat whenever I want. Come to my office. I can't have the guests wondering why some slick banker type has come to call on us."

Once we were seated in my office, Garrett looked around. "Not much."

"I don't get a fancy office like you do to show off to buyers. Only the staff come in here so I can call them out for their poor performance."

"Ha, you're no boss. You're too soft for that. You hear from your ma?"

"She's well, as is Maggie. And if you make me wait one more second for news on my property, I'll strangle ya, pack you in a crate, and ship it back to Dublin so you can see them for yourself."

"Would be nice to see home." He held up a hand to stop my protests. "And it's not your land…yet. The owners want to sell, and your price was acceptable to them."

"Yes." My chest swelled as if inflated with a helium balloon, and I slapped my hand on the table. "When do they want to make the deal?"

"Now don't flip your wig. There's a complication. The family that inherited the land owes back taxes on it, and they can't just sell it. It's got to go to court and through all the hoops." Garrett looked me in the eye. "I won't lie to you. It can be a long process. Maybe years."

The balloon deflated.

"Years?" My dreams sped away from me, out of my reach. With that an itch that I could never satisfy reared up.

"Listen, I have an idea." A sly smile spread across Garrett's mug. "The local magistrate has women problems. His wife doesn't understand him. See? And the man has needs. And ol' Garrett, the land agent, I might just be able to find ladies to meet those needs."

"Please stop there." I stood and looked out my small

window. It had no view as it came against the hill, with just a small path behind it. My view was of tree roots. But it was clean soil, in clean land, in beautiful country. I would own a piece of it. "Is there any other plot of land that would work?"

"None that I know of. All the lakefront land is being snatched up by bigshots like your boss. I don't see how you'll make a go of it. What with your employer expanding his resorts." Garrett put out his cigarette and lit another.

"Because there are plenty of people who won't be able to afford that new place. People who want to get their children out of the squalor of the city for a few weeks over the summer. A small working dairy farm, with simple meals. No fancy shows, no full orchestras."

"Like what we got on the other side of the hill?"

"Yes, but not for Irish."

"You're going to build it for the Jews?"

"For anyone. Our places are simple, but if you don't know how to dance the *céilí* then you can't join in the fun. And here, they have their big circle dances. But what if it were just for Americans? What if we had a library where kids could continue their schoolwork over the summer? So they were even smarter when school started again."

My dream. The path toward never depending on another man for my bread. Just as I had saved enough to start it, it was slipping away again.

"You and your schooling. For a man who stopped his learning at how to do sums, you're doing just fine for yourself."

"That's only because I refuse to give up. I've already waited years. There is always something standing in my way. The Irish can't do this. A poor man can't do that. You need an education, connections, money. Well, now I have money. Taxes. It comes down to stupid taxes."

"I can connect you with investors, people who will give you money to open one of those big resorts. With your reputation, you'll be rolling in dough."

"I don't take loans. I won't owe anyone anything. Speaking of which." I pulled out my wallet. "I was just at the bank, I can pay you your fee."

He held up his hand. "No fee for you, especially as there's no deal completed."

"I don't want to owe you anything. Anything more than I already do. If you hadn't found me that job over on the other side…" I held out a stack of bills to him, but he pushed my hand away.

"For that you certainly don't owe me. You're not in my debt. Don't concern yourself. Besides, I know how to collect when the time comes. You've got a nice secure job here, with steady pay. I trust you."

"I won't have my nice steady job if you don't get your keister out." I waved him toward the door.

"Old Bergen has you on a string, eh?"

"Old Bergen's been good to me. Showing me the ropes, giving me a chance."

"You and I both know he's no saint." Garrett nudged me with his elbow.

Fear clenched my gut.

"Hush, everyone bought from the black market during the war." I stopped Garrett from entering the public area to make sure he wasn't going to blab about some of Bergen's under-the-table dealings for food and supplies that were not necessarily in our rations.

"Don't worry. I keep everyone's secrets." Garrett tapped himself on the chest.

"Like the local magistrate's?"

"Pshw. Every decent man keeps his wife away from the magistrate. That's no secret. And believe me, there are some things you're better off not knowing." Garrett placed his hat on his head and meandered out into the lobby.

I kept an eye on him, just to be safe. He had bigger and possibly more legal ways to earn his money these days. But old habits die hard. I would never hang him for it. If it weren't for him, I would have been completely lost when Da died.

Getting crushed by the machines he was supposed to be fixing was bad enough. But leaving his widow and kids with debt to the factory bosses was beyond tragic. I shook the memory of that shanty town the factory called "laborers housing." That company owned everything from the bed we slept in to the clothes we wore. And the death benefits consisted of a pine box in the field. When the factory bosses own the cemetery, that should be the clue not to work there. Garrett got me set up with a job at the Irish resorts as a building engineer. Helped me find passage for Ma and Mags to go back to Ireland. He was a fixer. And now that he worked for a legitimate land agent, he was still fixing things.

And keeping people's secrets.

We probably all had secrets, even Mr. Bergen. After all, I wasn't particularly forthcoming with my boss about my plans. *Keep your head down, work hard.* Da had been right about that. He made the mistake of thinking he could spend his life working hard for someone else. I was going to be my own man. What had seemed like months away now stretched to years. Giving up wasn't an option, but my frustration might overtake my patience.

Chapter 2

CATHY

"You're going to have to get dressed. You can't mope in the room for the next two weeks," Marilyn huffed. She wore a wrap dress beautifully. But on me it looked like an empty sack.

"I might as well stay here the rest of my life." The five hours since the disastrous car ride felt like five years. I rolled over on my bed and faced away from her.

"Who stays in the Catskills their entire life?" She pulled me up. "You're only going to make it worse if you don't show up. Daddy will truly lock you away then."

I allowed my efficient and well-meaning sister to dress me. She was right; hiding away would only make it worse. I clung to a shred of hope that if Daddy got the job snatched away, maybe he could ask to have the job given back. He could explain it was some kind of misunderstanding.

"Stop doing that. The dress will just have to lay flat." I reached in and pulled out all the hankies she stuffed down the front to try to give me a shape I would never have.

"You'll never catch Will Hartman's eye that way."

"Let's hope I don't." I grabbed my clutch purse and tapped my toe while she applied her lipstick one more time. "Come on. I want to get it over with. A few dances, I'll say

I'm tired from the sun, and come back to the room to sleep."

The gravel paths were already empty as we followed the sound of the band to the main ballroom. The lake was a black empty space between the resort and the moonlit trees. Every single person staying at Pine Breeze had beaten us there. Crushing together on the dance floor, or laughing and drinking overly sweet punch along the side of the room. The noise and crowd were almost enough to send me scurrying back. Only, the others spotted me before I could make a getaway.

"I hear your graduation party was a gas." Will approached me and took my arm.

"Daddy always makes a fuss."

Silence lasted a moment longer than comfortable. Talk between Will and me hadn't been easy since he returned from Guam.

"Thanks again for writing me back. Getting mail was what kept us going."

"Of course I'd write to you. It was the least I—we could do." I looked into his deep brown eyes, which had lost some of the light from when we played here as kids.

He cleared his throat. "I've got a great job lined up at my uncle's insurance company. He's giving me all the humdinger accounts right from day one." The crinkle in his eyes returned, a remnant of his old self. I had hoped the happy Will would come back from the war. For the most part, he did. He'd make someone a good husband. Just not me. "I know you'd like a job in insurance, too. Gosh, Cathy, you're smarter than any of the fellows I met at the company. Maybe I can put in a good word for you. It would be fine for you to work until…"

I knew what he was saying. Knew that everyone expected Daddy to support me until I married someone. And everyone assumed that someone was Will.

The band played a lively Lindy Hop. I put on a brave face and joined Will in the dance.

The song stopped abruptly, and I knocked into him from the momentum of the sugar push step.

"Ow." I rubbed my knee after it bumped into his shin.

"You okay?"

"I think I'll sit out the next one." I nodded to the edge of the room, indicating that I'd wait there.

The sweat on my brow and rapid heartbeats weren't from the dance. If Will thought I was desperate to get out of my house, he would see opportunity.

He might propose any minute. I would hurt him by turning him down, and he didn't deserve to be hurt. If I could avoid the question entirely, then I wouldn't need to worry about trading Daddy's well-meaning protection for Will's.

I pressed my back against the outer wall, which was marginally cooler than the packed ballroom. Will went in search of a drink as I attempted to filter out the chatter and focus on the music.

Not far away in the corner, Mr. Cullen surveyed the room. His keen eyes took note of every detail, but a casual smile never left his face.

His traveling scrutiny caught my stare and instead of shyly looking away, I met his gaze.

His smile turned warmer. My heartbeat revved even higher. I took his smile as an invitation to approach him. Mr. Cullen was interesting, different.

"You're not dancing?" he asked as I neared close enough that conversation was possible.

"I was. Can't you tell?" I dabbed my brow, not really caring that I drew attention to my perspiration. Something about Mr. Cullen was safe.

"I merely thought you glowed with health." His smile increased.

"Mr. Cullen, do all the ladies like those empty compliments?" I returned the wink I'd been holding for him since this afternoon, when my career was just starting instead of ending before it even took off.

"Many don't think they're empty compliments."

"Hmmm." I stood next to him, comfortably glancing around. "Do you ever get bored of it?"

"Of what?"

"All the *fun*."

He chuckled. "You say 'fun' as if it were poison."

I couldn't help but feel those butterflies in my belly again. His chuckle was deep and sincere. Not the polite laugh of a resort manager being kind to a guest. I didn't want to come off as a stick in the mud, moping on the sidelines.

"It seems frivolous to be dancing when there's so much trouble in the world," I said.

"Maybe dancing is the only way to cope with the

tragedies of the time." His words struck my heart. Earlier, I'd been sulking about the loss of a job, but now, reflecting on the greater loss so many had endured gave me some perspective. Thomas Cullen made having fun seem like the antidote for my pain.

"Dance?" I waved my arm toward the crowd. I didn't care if I was being too forward. He was worth the risk.

"I generally don't dance." His reply was so quiet, I almost didn't catch it.

"Surely if you wanted to, it wouldn't be against the rules."

"Mr. Bergen's very kind, and allows the staff many freedoms to enjoy the resort."

"Then why don't you dance?"

"Not many people want to partner with me." His right hand had been tucked into his pocket in a most natural pose. When he revealed the hand, the top portions of his four fingers were missing. Quickly, he shoved his hand back. "Sorry. I didn't mean to offend you."

I said nothing. I'd seen so many injuries in men of his age. War had a way of normalizing what was previously shocking.

I extended my left hand. "I'm available for the next dance." I didn't pose it as a question this time.

He hesitated but took my hand in his. I forced myself not to recoil at the sensation of fingers that ended shy of where they should.

The band chose that moment for a fox-trot, the most boring dance in the world. I wanted my dance with Mr.

Cullen to be energetic, to feel my heart race.

He swept me onto the floor. Despite the mass of people, space opened for us. Swirling in time, I barely had to keep my feet on the ground. His strong arms effortlessly guided me. I didn't need up-tempo music to make my heart race. Dancing was fun, but dancing with a partner who had spent hours studying others in the act made the experience exhilarating. He had a degree in dancing and I could learn from him.

His eyes never left mine, and yet we never collided with another pair. Thrilling jolts radiated from my heart. The fatigue from earlier vanished. The smile that sat on my lips was a reflection of my whole being.

"Now you look like you're enjoying the Catskills," Mr. Cullen said as we made the turn.

"I do love it here. The clean air, the woods. I just don't always like the crowds." I nodded toward the center of the dance floor.

"Then you must have appreciated the new site Mr. Bergen showed you today." We glided across as a path opened up and Mr. Cullen twirled me.

A laugh escaped my chest at the dizzying sensation. "The place was breathtaking. But I'm afraid it will soon look like any old resort. I'd love a simple place where families can play outside and just listen to the sounds."

"You would?" He cocked his head to the side and the angle of his jaw appeared even more masculine than before. A small patch of his beard where he missed shaving became visible.

I was going to protest his surprise when the orchestra stopped. People ceased dancing and applauded. But Mr. Cullen held me as if the music were going to start immediately again. A flash of confusion crossed his face and he released my hand and stepped back.

"That was a lovely dance. Thank you, Miss Gold."

"Can you call me Cathy?" My breathing was heavy from exertion.

"Is that short for Caitrin?"

"No. It's short for Catherine."

"That's what I said. Caitrin." He narrowed his eyes but a smile played at his lips.

"Is that Catherine in Irish?"

"Gaelic." He bowed.

"I never liked Catherine. But the way you say it sounds how it was meant to be said."

"Then it will be my name for you. And please call me Thomas." His smile bordered on mischievous.

"Not Tommy?" I mocked his tone.

"Never Tommy." The glee disappeared from his face. "But I'll answer to almost anything you call me. I have to make my rounds." He nodded and strode out of the ballroom.

My view of his retreating back was obscured when Will and the others appeared. Seeing them brought back the reality of my situation. I had to marry Will or stay at my parents' house, waiting for something, or really, someone better. No adventure awaited me. I was doomed to follow the path that everyone else had.

No one questioned me on my dance with Thomas. Thinking of his name brought back the thrill of our fox-trot, his strong arms expertly guiding me. Just a few minutes before, I had been so sure that all I wanted was a career and my life had no room for a husband. But a man was different than a husband. Just because I was choosing a career didn't mean I had to give up on passion. Love and a career, a man and a job. Everyone knew I was unconventional. The confusion he left me with muddled my brain. Or maybe made it clearer.

***

THOMAS

I had danced with guests before. Mostly older women and very young girls. It was expected as part of my duties to mingle; "schmooze" was the word Mr. Bergen used. And I could turn up the charm whenever it was needed.

But with Caitrin, no false charm needed. She was stunningly beautiful. That was true, but she had more than looks. Many stunningly beautiful women had graced Pine Breeze before. Her brazen approach to me from the other end of the room caught my interest. Her disregard for my deformity connected me to her. But her love of the mountains meant the most. Others were more concerned with what could be built here, rather than appreciate the perfection nature had already built.

When I glanced at the clock in the office, it dawned on me that if I didn't take five minutes to answer Ma's letter, I'd never get a chance. Prodding the kitchen staff to move faster would have to wait, as I nearly jogged to my office at the back of the resort.

I had just written that I was so proud of Maggie and her studies in French. I suggested that she might find work as a translator in London one day, when Mr. Bergen entered.

I stood immediately folding the letter away. "I was just sitting for a moment, sir."

He dismissed my apology with a wave. "I'm not worried about you working hard, son. You're the strongest back I have around here. And my most trusted." He sat in the wooden chair on the other side of my desk and motioned me to take my seat. The past year had been rough on him. Losing a son was much harder than losing a father.

With most employers, they beckoned workers to their big fancy offices to make sure everyone understood who was in charge. But Mr. Bergen didn't lord his power. He was commanding, to be sure. You don't get to be the owner of not one, but two, summer resorts without acting the boss. Yet he wasn't power hungry or consumed with profit like some business owners who sucked the life right out of their workers.

"I saw our mutual friend, Garrett, here earlier." He let the statement hang.

"Yes, he was here on a personal errand for me. Nothing to do with Pine Breeze."

Bergen tilted his head to the side. "You're a grown man and allowed your privacy. But if you need something, I hope you'll come to me."

"I'm hoping one day to start my own business. A small inn." I held my breath. I couldn't afford to offend him, not financially, not in any way.

A series of expressions crossed his face until he settled on a sad smile with a glistening in his eyes. "I figured we couldn't keep someone like you forever."

"I'm still a long way from being able to start. I send much of my pay to my family. Besides, I won't leave you shorthanded. When I have the money, I'll remain with you until the end of the season." The taste of being my own boss sat at the tip of my tongue. But I never got a belly full of it.

He nodded. "I know you would. As for Garrett, I wouldn't have been able to keep the place running without him these past few years. Still, might be best if he used the service entrance, all the same. I don't trust him completely."

"That's a wise stance. I'll make sure he doesn't come here again. If I need to meet him, I'll do it somewhere else."

"I appreciate that."

Silence ensued, and I waited as he tapped his fingertips together.

"I'm glad you were dancing with Catherine Gold. She's the moody middle daughter, and sometimes takes a little extra coaxing to come out of her shell. Mr. Gold has told me he doesn't know what to do with her. She has some notion about moving far away on her own, and all he wants is for her to be safe in these crazy times."

"A son is a son until he takes him a wife, a daughter is a daughter all of her life."

"That some Irish *mishegas*?"

"Yes, sir."

"Anyway, if Cathy Gold is happy, her father is happy.

And if her father is happy his money is likely to flow to the new Belvedere. It only took you two years of working for me before I noticed your genius."

"You're too kind, Mr. Ber—"

"None of that Paddy charm on me. You're brilliant and if you were born in some other circumstances, you'd probably be sitting where I am. But never mind that. As smart as you are, the Belvedere is an enormous undertaking."

"And it's not my Irish *mishegas* when I say I'm honored by the trust you put into me." I wouldn't revel in this accomplishment since I only got the position because Larry Bergen died in Europe. "I won't let you down."

His eyes filled up, but he recovered quickly. "I'm about to make your job even harder."

I waited until he was done rubbing the edge of my worn desk with his index finger. Something was on his mind, and I wasn't going to interrupt the man who had just paid me a compliment and reassured me of the trust he was placing in me.

"You've met my boy, Ron."

"A fine lad."

"No he's not." He sighed. "I'd hoped the army would have put some sense into him. But he was hardly there long enough. Who knew a broken toe could heal so crooked he couldn't wear boots? Two weeks in basic training and he came home needing custom shoes. Four months later, we heard Lawrence…"

Mr. Bergen rose from his seat to wander the small

office. I remained sitting because I was sure we weren't done. "I had nothing growing up. My parents got off that boat with two candlesticks and the name of a distant relative to stay with. I'm sure your folks were the same."

"Minus the candlesticks."

We shared a laugh.

"My father scrabbled for every nickel. Saved enough so I didn't have to do factory work. Gave me enough to start my own business. One business led to another. I was lucky, I was quick. And now Pine Breeze. When my sons came along, I never wanted them to know a day without meat on the table. I had no idea how to raise wealthy kids. Larry was okay. Ron is spoiled."

"You're a good father. You provide for your family."

"I provided a little too much. But now I want to try to fix it if I can. Do you see? I want Ron to work. To work at the Belvedere with you."

A hard hot lump of anger clogged my throat. I was the one with the knowledge and Ron only came to the job from the bad luck of his older brother dying in the war. I managed to tamp down the injustice to say, "I'm happy to work for the younger Mr. Bergen. I'm fortunate that you would keep me on." If I had to bow and scrape before that snot, I would do it, but only until the second I could make my own dreams happen, which now seemed years away.

"For crying out loud, man. Do you think I'd put my idiot son in charge of my most important business? No, he's going to be your assistant manager. He's got to learn the ropes in order to inherit the business."

"Oh." I wish I could say that relief caused my lack of words. Instead, it occurred to me that the only thing worse than working *for* Ronald Bergen was having Ronald Bergen work for me.

"I don't expect miracles, Thomas. And I appreciate your discretion in this." He paced back over to my desk and could look me in the face again, after having made this confession. "To motivate him, I'm cutting off his allowance and he'll only have what he earns at work. I trust you to knock whatever sense you can into the boy."

"Again, I am honored and humbled by your faith in me."

"Faith in each other is all we have sometimes." His gaze drifted to the window and the black night outside.

Considering what we'd recently discovered about what humanity was capable of, I wasn't sure I had faith in people, let alone the Almighty. And since He hadn't made any impact on Ron yet, I doubted I could do any better.

Chapter 3

CATHY

"You're not paying attention. Are you?" Marilyn demanded as we paddled our canoe along the shore.

"Sorry, I was distracted." I'd slept in fits and starts. Still reliving the agonizing moment Daddy told me he'd taken my job away. I barely spoke to my parents at breakfast, not that I was really punishing anyone except myself. I'd agreed to go for a canoe ride with Marilyn to avoid facing others.

"I was asking your opinion about caterers. David wants to use his cousin."

"That sounds nice." I scanned the shoreline, trying to glimpse a flash of red hair.

"Really? Nice? This is the guy who served chopped liver and called it pâté. Who are you looking for?"

"No one." I faced her. She didn't need to know that Thomas Cullen's face was the only comforting image I held on to as I lay in bed last night.

"Is it Will? Would you really turn him down?" Marilyn stopped paddling and let her hand trail in the water. "He's strong and kind. And he's got a good job in the city."

"I don't love him." I placed my paddle in the canoe and we drifted. "And even if I did, I can't get married now."

"You want to live with Mom and Dad?"

"No, being away at school gave me that taste of freedom."

"That's why I want my own house."

"But it won't be your own house. It will be David's house."

Marilyn splashed water at me. "You're being silly. I think you took those women in history classes too seriously."

I rolled my eyes. It wasn't the history classes that got me. It was the math classes. And Marilyn knew that. There had to be something out there that would grab my interest, other than a household budget. The stifling noose of marriage was the only thing less appealing than living under my father's roof.

"I could live in one of those women's boardinghouses they have in the city. Daddy can't stop me from getting every job in New York."

"Just every decent well-paying job. You'd only be able to afford some tenement room." She wrinkled her nose.

"Daddy started out in a tenement room."

"Exactly why he'll never let you go there. That's what donating money is for. To help the refugees."

"I need to do something. I sat out the entire war, watching other girls serve the country. Where's my adventure?"

She sighed. "Have Will take you somewhere exotic on a honeymoon." Marilyn picked up her paddle and started for the dock.

My stomach pitched at the thought of a honeymoon

with Will. The way everyone talked about Will and me like we were destined for each other, it made me feel as though I couldn't even choose my own husband.

It wasn't a husband I was looking for, anyway. It was freedom, adventure, and maybe a little risk to put some excitement into my life.

We paddled back to the dock to put the boat away before moving on to the next "fun activity."

As we neared the boathouse, I spied Thomas talking to the boy who took care of the boating equipment. He was lecturing him on some point about the shed when we pulled alongside, and he bent to grab the edge so we could get out safely.

"Did you ladies enjoy yourselves?"

"It was very peaceful," I replied.

"Too peaceful. David said he'll meet us for sack races. Come on." Marilyn motioned for me to follow.

"I think I'll stay here."

"Here?" She eyed me and then Thomas.

I narrowed my eyes and we exchanged silent communication that sisters shared. Resigned, she sighed, "I'll see you back in the room." She dashed off to find David.

"Are you looking to rest after paddling, Caitrin?" Thomas asked as he escorted me off the dock, his voice a friendly, soft tune that melted with the lap of the water.

"Not at all. I'm tired of company."

"Then I'll leave you." His polite smiled stayed in place, but his voice became cool.

"Oh, not your company. Just my sister's. And all my

friends." Without weighing the risks, I took his arm. I could be just as flirty as I wanted with a man who made me curious. "I mean, I'm sure you're working and busy."

"Why don't you come with me as I make my rounds of the outdoor facilities? It's the best part of my job, walking the grounds in this summer sun. The playing fields, the beach, the tennis courts."

He was dressed more casually today. A pair of pants and a white shirt that opened at the neck, exposing his collarbone. Thomas was my choice of whom to be with this afternoon, a little excitement, something novel in a typical Catskills day.

"Tell me why you're tired of your sister." Thomas strolled beside me, his head bent toward mine as if we were dearest friends.

"She's too preoccupied with her wedding for much other conversation."

"I imagine it's an important event for her."

"David is a fine boy. And Marilyn will be very happy with him."

"But…"

"But I know I wouldn't be. Not with David. I mean not with anyone." I shook my head. "I sound dopey."

We rounded the fields where three-legged races were starting. Thomas stopped to take in the activity, his critical eye roaming, calculating the number of guests, the staff's enthusiasm. He seemed to approve so we moved on.

"You sound like a young woman who wants to choose her own path. Sometimes choice is a burden instead of a gift."

"That would be a wise saying if I felt I had choices."

"Let's assume you do. What would you choose?"

"I want to work, and live on my own. But Daddy won't allow that. He took away the one chance I had and made it clear he'd stop me from living anywhere other than his home."

"You don't like your home?"

"Oh, it's a real humdinger." I mimicked Marilyn assessing the quality of the tablecloths for the wedding. "We have all the latest kitchen appliances. Our furniture is made of the softest materials. Our dishes are china and from the finest Fifth Avenue shops."

"You want simpler things." His hold on my arm tightened slightly as we crossed an uneven stone path.

"I want my own things. I want to come and go as I please." I took a breath. "You must think I'm a real chucklehead." To someone who had to work hard for a living, whining about wanting to work for a living had to sound like a spoiled brat.

"No, I like being my own man. I'm independent to a certain extent. I answer to no one but Mr. Bergen. My wages are mine to do with as I see fit. I imagine you also want to feel the dignity in work."

"Exactly, the dignity of work." I let the phrase roll around my mind.

He surveyed the beach. His frown led me to think he spied something that would require his correction. The play of emotions across his face showed his indecision. He nodded for us to proceed. Apparently, walking with me won out over whatever infraction he noted.

"So what would you do?" he asked.

"Actuarial science."

Thomas stopped at the edge of the tennis courts. They weren't in use now and the path wound around to where the woods started. He released my arm so he could look at me square on, but his hand brushed against my side as he pulled away, leaving a trail of heat.

"I think you lapsed into another language." He grinned.

I laughed and leaned against a tree for support. It wasn't every day that a man was attentive when I talked about my interests. Especially a man no one would approve of. A man whom I didn't already know everything about from who his parents were to what he had liked to eat for lunch in elementary school. "Actuarial science is the study of mathematics applied to risk."

"You'll have to explain more." He leaned against the fence that bordered the tennis courts, crossed his arms, and adopted a pose that was both challenging and inviting.

"Let's say you're an insurance company and you are going to offer a life insurance policy for someone. If you know his age, work, and health, you can estimate how long he'll live and, from that, determine how much he should pay."

"No one knows how long he'll live." His eyes turned the shade of the blue of the lake, and I felt like I was floating in water.

"No one knows. But we can guess." I swallowed,

focusing on the part of my brain that held my intelligence, not the part that wouldn't let go of Thomas's eyes, not to mention his strong arms and confident smile. "And we can guess what will happen in the stock market and almost anything in future years. Using math and statistics."

"Caitrin, you might be brilliant with your fancy numbers, but there is one thing I know for sure. Based on what has happened in the stock market and people dying, we can't know what's going to happen the next minute, let alone the next years."

He pushed off the fence and came to stand next to me on the narrow path. His face was so close that I could detect the stubble of his beard, smell his clean minty scent, and feel the heat from his chest radiate to mine. Risk, excitement.

No numbers could have predicted the kiss I gave him. I pressed my lips over his, grabbing his shirt in my fists and pulling him against me. I'd kissed boys before. But this was kissing a man. He gasped and parted his lips slightly, and my tongue swept inside.

His body relaxed into mine and he cradled my head in his hand. His moan vibrated through me.

A virtuous girl wouldn't have gripped his shoulders and held on until she thought she'd pass out from not breathing. I'd left virtue back in the boathouse.

He must have lost his wind too, because he abruptly pulled away and stepped back, allowing the breeze to come between us.

The shock on his face only made his eyes more handsome. That bewildered expression endeared him to me even more than the passionate kiss. Here was my adventure, my risk. A man who was unknown and who was just as curious about me as I was about him.

***

THOMAS

"I'm sorry." I worked to steady my breathing. My God, I'd never risked my future on a bird and I didn't want to start. *She could have her dad throw me out on my ear.*

"Why are you sorry? I kissed you. Maybe I shouldn't have." She looked down at her feet and her voice became small as a blush appeared in her cheeks. "Do you want to forget it happened?"

"I couldn't ever forget your kiss. But I would never say anything. I'll take it to my grave."

She laughed uneasily. "You don't have to be that dramatic. It was only a kiss." Her voice faltered.

Only a kiss. She didn't seem like the type of woman who gave her kisses freely. I motioned for her to proceed on the path, in the direction where there would be plenty of people around, and we wouldn't risk privacy again.

I stood straighter and took a step back. "I'll do my best to give you a wide berth, if you want. I don't want you to feel uncomfortable."

"Oh, Thomas. You're the one person I feel comfortable with in this entire place." Her voice was quiet again, barely audible over the cries of victory coming from the field races. It held a sadness, a tone I hadn't heard from her before. "I'll join my friends."

And she strode to the group of young people jumping

in delight.

When Mr. Bergen asked me to make sure Cathy Gold was happy, he didn't mean for me to kiss her at the edge of the wood. And he certainly didn't mean for me to kiss her at the edge of the wood and then vow to avoid her.

My manners were failing. But then everything seemed to fail around Caitrin Gold. I chose to overlook the sloppy arrangement of beach chairs in order to spend more time walking with her. I put my entire future at risk so I could kiss her.

Da would have said she was a *Tuath Dé Danann* fairy sent to beguile me. To test me and prove my worth. If a pretty girl could so easily cause me to lose sight of my goal, I was doomed before I even bought the land, let alone built on it and opened a business.

I stalked back to the beach and took my frustrations out on the poor beach attendant. He didn't deserve the upbraiding I gave him. But better to lash out at him than to find Caitrin, take her in my arms, tip her head back, and show her how "comfortable" I could make her.

"Mr. Cullen." Sam bellowed my name as his lazy gait would never get him close enough to me to use a normal tone of voice.

"Sam, you can't be yelling like a banshee from across the beach. If you need me, use the legs the good Lord gave you to carry your carcass to me and speak your mind in a civil volume."

Sam's blank expression told me all I needed to know about this young man's future.

"Well?" I waited for the gears in his head to start grinding out a thought.

"There's a call for you."

I took a deep breath. "And did you get this someone's name?"

"Um."

I waved him off and nearly trotted to the main building. I'd already wasted plenty of time this morning. Trying to get water from the stone that was Sam's head would be pointless.

I took the veranda stairs two at a time and grabbed the phone from behind the front desk, earning a raised eyebrow from Mr. Bergen, who was greeting guests as they checked in.

"Thomas Cullen speaking."

"It's your old pal Garrett."

"Mr. Smith, so good of you to call. Has the…cream order been filled?"

"Ahh, our upstanding patriotic citizen Bergen is there. No, your *cream order* isn't filled. The magistrate's wife insisted they move to Florida, where her sister is, and his secretary isn't."

I turned farther away from Mr. Bergen, his intuitive ears, and the buzz in the lobby. "That's too bad. What does that mean for…future orders?"

"It means we're starting from scratch with a whole new magistrate. One I don't know."

"I see." My blood pressure, already high from kissing a beautiful guest and a jog to the main building, shot even higher. I fought to keep the dizziness at bay.

"Bit of a gamble at this point. But I always roll a seven. So don't worry your bright red head about it. Garrett's on the case. That does buy you a little extra time to gather your lettuce."

"That is good news. Uh, thank you for calling." I cradled the receiver. And came face-to-face with Bergen.

"Cream?"

"Mr. Smith's cows are sick. Pox, I think. Anyway, no cream from him. We'll have to find another supplier. I'll let the chef know to stick with meat dishes."

He nodded and placed a hand on my shoulder. "Tell Garrett to stay clear of my cream and anything else. I don't want you in too deep with him. Are you sure I can't lend you some money? Maybe we can arrange an investment. I would place my money on any business you start."

Alarm bells rang in my head. No loan, no investors, no debt to anyone. Bergen might be kindhearted and good intentioned, but no one would own me or my business. "I appreciate your faith and concern. I've got to do this on my own. You've helped me too much already. Besides, you need to make room for your son to take over."

"Hmm." Mr. Bergen's gaze traveled the expanse of the lobby. People milled about in bathing suits and tennis shorts. The laughter and high-pitched greetings juxtaposed the grim set of Bergen's mouth. "You can make deals with people that you regret. Be careful."

I thanked him, but didn't want to press further. No doubt, dealing on the black market had made an impression on Bergen's soul. But it wasn't like everyone else hadn't done it.

The rounds took less time than usual. Either because everything was running smoothly for once, or because my mind was preoccupied with other things. I was grateful to have some extra time to scrape together enough money to build. But if Garrett thought we were on shaky ground, that didn't give me comfort.

I checked in the heavily furnished library, and it was typically empty this time of day. We had an impressive full set of Encyclopedia Britannica. Mr. Bergen said that even though the books in the library might not get much use, a hotel full of Jewish people demanded that the books be there. "People of the book," he had said.

I grabbed the volume "A–Ad" and fumbled to spell "actuarial." I fumbled even more to understand the entry. It was as Caitrin said, using math to predict the future. I guess if mankind could obliterate an entire town with one bomb from an airplane, we could predict the future with math. Maybe if someone had used math to predict the Nazis, we could have avoided a whole mess of pain.

Not sure I'd want my future told to me. Of course, I wouldn't mind knowing what would happen to my land. It was dangerous thinking of it as my land already, but I couldn't help it. Caitrin Gold's kiss was even more unpredictable danger. I wondered if the numbers said the odds were in my favor.

Chapter 4

CATHY

I immersed myself in "fun" for the rest of the day. Even while playing tennis with Marilyn, I didn't dwell on the spot off to her right. The spot where I'd had the most amazing kiss of my life.

To be fair, I'd only had three other kisses. I didn't count the peck on the cheek from Bobby Simmons in third grade. He did that on a dare.

Most recently, Frank from Yale had kissed me a few times. He had a car that he somehow bought gas for and would come visit me. I would sneak out of the dormitory and we'd see a picture in town. In the back of the darkened theater we would kiss. I let him place his hands on my chest, but not under my blouse.

I wasn't sure why I stopped him. I wanted to feel what it would be like for a boy to touch me, but everything told me I had to say no. Frank moved on to Boston for work and I hadn't heard from him. I wasn't disappointed, except for not letting him touch my breasts.

"Daydreaming?" Mom asked as we waited to be seated for dinner.

"Tired. I think the tennis did me in."

"I'm glad you're back into the swing of things," Daddy

said as we followed the host to our table. "I've been worried about you."

Worried about me. The words were on the tip of my tongue to point out that he was the cause of my distress. But a scowl from Marilyn kept me quiet. Fine, let her be the favorite. It wasn't like everyone didn't already think I was fickle and would change my mind.

I scanned the room, as I had been scanning every place. But Thomas was doing a good job of not being where I was. That hurt way more than Frank's disappearance.

"What looks good tonight?" Daddy asked.

The menu varied slightly, but the same roast chicken, kugel, and variations on liver had been served since I could remember. Except for a few years of extreme rations when there was quite a lot of salad.

"I'll have chicken." I tossed the menu on the table, rattling the bread dish.

"I thought you were done moping." The teasing tone in Daddy's voice didn't take the sting out of what he said.

"It's not moping, Daddy." I could barely keep tears from my eyes. "You took my job away from me."

"I'm protecting you. Come work for me. It'll be fun, the two of us taking the train into the city together. Your mother used to help me before you girls came along." His smile was sincere. He truly didn't understand my need for independence.

Mom's smile strained, and she patted Daddy's hand.

Mom never talked about her college experience. I know she'd met Daddy there, and they were both interested in law school. But only Daddy went since they got married right away after graduation. There's an old photograph of Mom pregnant with Marilyn, typing out Daddy's papers for law school. I suspected that Mom would have liked doing more than just having us girls.

With a monumental effort, I relaxed the muscles in my face and neck. I could have patience, but not endless amounts. At some point, Daddy was either going to give in to my wishes, or I would do something drastic just to show I could make my own decisions. However rash they might be.

Marilyn's fiancé, David, and his family joined us at the large table and dinner got under way. Waiters and busboys dashed madly about. The din of clanking silverware and loud voices made the food go down in clumps. But the entire time, I practiced my mom face. It's the polite expression of someone too intelligent to bother with the conversation, but whose duty requires that they do.

I begged off dessert, saying I needed a little fresh air. Mom offered to come with me.

Once outside on the veranda, we stepped away from the dining hall and the noise.

"Thanks," I said.

"I know you want to work for an insurance company, or maybe something on Wall Street. Filing Daddy's paperwork isn't your idea of interesting."

"Why did he even bother sending me to college? I should have just been—" I held my breath, realizing the mistake I made.

Mom laughed. "A housewife?" She wandered over to

the railing and looked up at the clear night sky. "Education is important to us. And we had daughters. I don't think he could have tolerated not sending you to college. Especially when all his friends were sending their sons to Harvard and such." She pulled me to her side. "We're all just so fortunate that we're alive, and well, and all together this summer."

"Except for Beth. Are you picking her up from the station?"

"Daddy and I are borrowing Mr. Bergen's car and driver tomorrow. I miss her."

"Me too." Only I didn't really. She was okay as far as little sisters go. But she fit in even less than I did, and I could never understand the things she was passionate about. And Beth was passionate about everything.

"Try to understand what your father's concerns are." Mom wrapped her arm around me.

"Will he try to understand mine? I can't marry Will. You know that, right?"

She nodded. "I wouldn't have you marry someone you didn't love. Do you really dislike us so much that you don't want to live with us?"

"It's not that. I need my own life. I want to work for myself. Make my own money. Have the dignity that comes from work. That job would have given me that independence."

She stared into the night, and I hoped this would be the moment she told me about her decisions. Because she'd also graduated from college near the top of her class. I prayed that she would share what had happened to her dreams, if she had any.

Thomas Cullen stepped out of the shadows carrying two plates of cake slices. If someone had to interrupt us, I was glad it was him. "Did you lovely ladies miss out on Mrs. Nussbaum's famous marble cake?"

"We did. Although I'm not sure I have room for it." Mom smiled warmly. "I think I'll go in and curl up with my book. Good night, Mr. Cullen. Good night, Cathy. Don't stay out too late, you had a long day." Mom turned and disappeared into the main lobby, taking her secrets with her.

"You didn't have to bring me cake," I said even as I took the plate he offered.

"I saw you and your mother leave the dining room before dessert and wanted to check on you."

"I didn't see you there."

"I know. I didn't… Not even when you were playing tennis with your sister… I…"

"Thomas Cullen, have you been spying on me all afternoon?" I tried my best Betty Grable pose and hoped I looked alluring and not as if I were playacting.

"It's my job to see to all areas of the resort. If I happened to be examining the same place you were enjoying, that was merely coincidental." His charming smile made my heart skip a beat. Then his face became serious. "But one word from you and I promise not to look for you ever again."

My mouth went dry and I tried to answer. Regaining my composure, I said, "The resort is big, but not large enough to avoid each other." A few eyelash flickers and I was out of charming moves.

"That's the only reason we'll see each other? Running into one another at the ping-pong table?" His Cheshire grin brought forth the silly giggle I'd been trying to tamp down.

A seductive woman shouldn't giggle. "I don't play ping-pong. I like the outdoors better."

"Hmmm. So do I. Then we'll see each other in Mother Nature's finery." He dipped his head and strode back into the building.

I took a forkful of the cake, but it wasn't the sweet chocolaty bite that made my throat hum. Thomas Cullen did things to me that no boy had ever awakened. Maybe it was the uncertainty of what I would be doing next month, or the fact that peace brought a confidence that war couldn't allow. But I was feeling ready for an adventure.

If I couldn't shake off the chains of my father's expectations, I could at least decide who I shared my affections with. It certainly wouldn't be Will Hartman. I at least had control over my own heart. And maybe a little bit of a bad reputation would drive Will away. Would drive all the boys away. Would wake Daddy up to the fact that he couldn't dictate my life.

Chapter 5

THOMAS

My da's voice echoed in my skull. "You're playing with fire, laddie." He would say that anytime I took an unnecessary risk. When I challenged the bullies in town who tried to relieve me of my pocket change. When I refused to work the factory floor when the lights went out and the dark made dangerous work a certain death. And when I attended that union meeting. Da was all for keeping his head down, doing an honest day's work, taking home the scraps, and being the obedient worker.

Look where that had landed him.

A world of difference existed between standing up to the bosses and flirting with the boss's niece. Or whatever Caitrin Gold was to Bergen. No matter the relation, I had no business spending time with her. No business spending time with a woman who wanted more from life than what was handed her. She was a striver and determined. Any other girl born to that privileged life would gladly accept the easy way. She got my blood pumping for sure.

So when I made my morning rounds of the beach, I didn't stop to talk to her as she sat on the edge of the crowd, a book resting on her lap, but her gaze directed out over the water. She was a true beauty. Her coffee-colored hair was forever coming loose and the stray locks brushed against her pale cheeks. In profile, her chin jutted out to show her determination. I pitied her father. Caitrin Gold would get what Caitrin Gold wanted.

Something stirred the air, and she turned, catching sight of me gaping.

A smart man would have nodded and moved on. I generally considered myself a smart man, but those brown eyes and determined chin washed all the brains out of me.

I didn't have to make any decision; she bounded up and trotted over to me.

"I knew we'd see each other again." Her smile lit her face and hit my gut.

"As you said, it's a small resort."

"Are you making your rounds? I'll go with you." She tucked her book under her arm and draped her towel over her shoulder.

"I don't remember inviting you," I said as I held out my arm. The natural way we fit together made it too easy to link arms and too difficult to keep my distance.

"You enjoy my company. Besides, I was bored of my book."

"True. I do enjoy your company." I led the way at a more leisurely pace than I would typically make my rounds. Having her arm through mine was a moment to be savored.

"Thomas, last night when you brought out that cake…" Her eyes searched my face.

"Caitrin, you're a lovely young woman. And I do enjoy your company. But you should be setting your sights on all these young men here. I've noticed one in particular who seems to fancy you."

"Will." Her voice dropped to a level mostly used to describe the singing talents of our latest act. "I don't want to talk about him. But when you came out last night, was it just to be nice to me and Mom?" The warmth of her side radiated to me. I could feel the pulse in her delicate wrist resting on my arm.

"I wish it had been. I wish I could say I was just doing my job. But I fancy you and I shouldn't." With great effort, I untwined our arms.

I barely took in the grounds. For all I knew, the crew could have left the grass un-mowed and the deck chairs broken. My eyes were on Caitrin's best side. The side still pressed against mine.

She sighed. "But I wouldn't want you to have been just doing your job. I want you to seek me out because you want to see me, not because I'm a guest."

As we were rounding the back side of the kitchen where the herb garden was hidden from view of the guests, she leaned over to peck me on the cheek.

Caught off guard, I abruptly stopped our progress.

"Thomas, I'd like to kiss you again. Really kiss you." She took my face in her hands and brought me down to her sweet lips.

A stronger man would have stopped her. A decent man would have said, "Catherine Gold, you are too young for me and we don't belong together."

But my flesh was as weak as any sinner's.

Our mouths parted and fit perfectly. Our tongues entwined and any brains in my head were completely swept away. Her soft moan vibrated off my chest. I pulled back.

"I need to see you more." Her breathless words could have been mine.

"We shouldn't. It's not right." I ran a finger along her jaw and tucked the stray bit of her curly hair behind heaven's perfectly crafted ear.

"You don't know me very well, Thomas Cullen, if you think I care about what's right."

I laughed and pulled her against me, because even those few inches were too much space for her to be away from me.

"Meet me at the boathouse early tomorrow morning. I'd like to take you somewhere. If that's okay."

"Thomas, I trust you to take me anywhere." She gave me a last sweet kiss and scampered off toward the main building.

I shoved my hands into my pockets and watched her form grow smaller and smaller. "Oh, Caitrin, don't trust a man who allows his brains to be washed away."

***

CATHY

My heart was positively jumping out of my chest as I gently pulled the closet door open. The squeak of the hinges wasn't enough to wake Marilyn, sound asleep in her bed.

Without looking outside, I knew it would be chilly. The sun was about an hour away from making an appearance over the lake, but I didn't want Thomas to wait for me. I didn't want another second to go by before I saw him.

Being so forward with a man had never occurred to me. Then again, Thomas Cullen had never crossed my path. I was itching for something exciting to do. And the scavenger hunt planned for later that day wasn't going to cut it.

Yesterday, when I'd turned and seen Thomas standing there staring at me, not even pretending to examine the grounds, exhilaration fluttered in my chest for the first time. I had thought the Catskills were no longer exciting. Boy, was I wrong.

I'd arrived at Pine Breeze confident I would start my new life as an independent woman. The childish games of past summers were barely entertaining.

Thomas Cullen and I were not playing a childish game. Grown, independent women have love affairs. When my future was snatched away, he offered me something I couldn't find in anyone else. Someone who was interested in my goals, someone who believed the same things I did, despite our differences.

I slipped into heavy trousers and buttoned up the one sweater I had packed. Feeling around on the floor for my oxfords I bumped my head and winced.

"What are you doing?" Marilyn mumbled from the other side of the room.

"I, uh, can't sleep. Thought I'd go to the library to read." I located my wayward shoe and stood up.

Marilyn switched on the bedside lamp and blinked. "You need a heavy sweater for the library?"

"It's cold in the morning." I considered putting on my lipstick, now that the light was on anyway.

Marilyn shifted up to rest against the headboard. She stared at me applying makeup. “You’re meeting someone.” She rubbed her face. “It can’t be Will.”

“I did meet someone. He’s so exciting. Don’t tell Mom and Daddy.” I blotted my lips with a hankie and took Marilyn’s chiffon scarf from the edge of the mirror to wrap around my neck. Not so much for warmth but the green brought out my eyes.

“Who is it?” She was fully awake and taking on her big sister role.

“Thomas Cullen.”

“The manager?”

“I was walking with him yesterday. And the day before.” I stood back from the vanity and grabbed my key. “And I kissed him,” I said under my breath before shuffling to the door.

Marilyn threw off the covers and came between me and the door. “You’re not really going out in the middle of the night to meet him?”

“Why shouldn’t I?” I could’ve pushed her out of the way. Even though she was my big sister, I had a few inches on her.

“I can’t let you ruin your reputation. Or break Daddy’s heart this way.” She pushed me back toward the center of the room. “I know you’re angry with him. Frankly, I think he’s going overboard, too. But doing something dangerous isn’t going to get back at him. It will only hurt you.”

“I trust Thomas. He’s a good man.”

“I don’t think you can trust a man like that.”

"Like what? And before you answer, don't say anything about his religion or status. Because Bubbe and Zayde were poor Jews on the Lower East Side not so long ago."

"Fine. But there's only one reason *any* man would plan to meet you in private." She put her hands on her hips and glared, working on her disapproving mother look for when she had children.

"Maybe we're both looking for a little summer adventure." I tossed my head.

"I don't think his idea of 'summer adventure' is the same as yours." Yet, her tone softened and her shoulders dropped as she stepped aside.

"If I'm not back before Mom and Daddy come by, cover for me."

"Don't do anything stupid," she called from her perch on the edge of her bed, watching me leave.

"Marilyn, I graduated top of my class."

"That's exactly what I'm afraid of."

I cringed when the squeak of the bungalow door hinges echoed in the still outdoors, but no one was on the path. Scurrying across the back lawn, I tried to keep to the trees. The expanse seemed even bigger when it was empty of the crowds.

I'd spent the previous evening reliving my kiss with Thomas, almost not wanting my cheese blintzes to pass over my lips, ruining the sensation that still lingered.

By the time I'd entered college, the war in Europe had been pretty much over. Boys had started coming home, and there was cautious optimism. But it wasn't until those awful bombs obliterated towns in Japan that we all truly felt safe again. That safety gave me the taste for adventure. That job in Philadelphia would have been my adventure. I couldn't let Daddy steal my chance to have some kind of excitement.

Thomas could provide me with at least a few days of thrill. Something that was my own, something that my parents couldn't keep me from. Maybe I'd find out what it meant to be a woman. Real adventure has some risk. I understood that, even if Marilyn thought I didn't. My reputation didn't matter to me. Daddy's opinion didn't matter to me. The only one I wanted to impress in the early morning was Thomas.

A shadow moved inside the boathouse. An unmistakable shadow. The lean lines of Thomas's arms hefted a rowboat down from the frame. His pleated trousers hid his form underneath, but the power he showed in handling the boat proved his strength.

"Hello, Thomas." I had meant my voice to be happy, but a breathless quality made his name seem like a secret whisper.

"So you did come, Caitrin. I thought maybe you'd changed your mind at a rendezvous with a strange man." His sly grin might have been an attempt at putting me off, but it made the sense of danger even more attractive.

"You're not strange. Just different. And I would never be so rude as to stand a boy up."

A gruff noise came from his throat. "A long time since someone called me a boy. But I'll take it as a compliment."

With a quiet splash, he shoved the boat into the water,

slipped the oars through the locks, and stepped nimbly in. He beckoned me with his outstretched left hand. Gingerly, I placed one foot in the wobbling boat. I was afraid to move farther in and cause the whole thing to topple over. Before I knew it, he had grabbed me around the waist and effortlessly placed me on the front-facing seat.

"You still haven't said where we're going." I pulled at the cuff of my sleeve. The reality of what I was doing had sunk in. I was on a near dark lake with a man, whose expectations I could guess. Marilyn's warning made more sense. But my stubborn side, and the quiver in my chest, pushed her words away.

"Just around that little island is a piece of land that I think someone with your sensibilities would appreciate." His arms worked the oars, each flex undulating in time with the movement of the boat. His grip with his right hand was weaker and he had to work twice as hard with that arm so we went in a straight line.

"My sensibilities?" My mouth went dry, but I wasn't going to back down. I might never get another chance like this again.

"You seem to love the natural world like I do. Too many buildings and people can get in the way of valuing it the way it should be."

"Is that why you asked me to come? To appreciate nature?" My belly clenched. My inexperience had read his signals wrong.

He set his jaw tight and dug in with extra effort to propel us even faster. "Might be that. Might be I wanted to spend some time alone with you. Without your father, without my boss. Just two…" He glanced at me, and with the sun rising behind my back, his face was washed in a pink glow, his blue eyes piercing through the glare.

"Two?" Hope returned with a flicker of that feeling from our last kiss.

He shrugged. "People who love nature." He grunted and turned around to determine our location. "Just past that bramble." He jutted out his chin to indicate our landing place.

A sloping expanse came into view. Spruce and birch dotted the land, and the morning calls of the birds welcomed us to the spot.

After a bit of maneuvering, we lightly bumped against the shore. Thomas got out and dragged the boat high enough so I wouldn't have to step into water. He flung a blanket over his shoulder and took my hand.

I let him lead me to the center, his rough hand holding mine tight enough to guide me but lightly enough that I wanted more pressure.

"Sit here and I'll tell you my plans." He indicated the rough wool blanket.

I sat and curled my legs under me. Thomas plopped down and stared at the lightening sky.

"This will be mine. I, Thomas William Cullen, will be a landowner. Something my da never dreamed possible. I'm going to run my own business, not answer to anyone. I'm going to turn this into an inn. Not a big fancy resort, but it's going to be a fine place. A simple place for families. Any family. To get out of the stink of the city and give their kids some of God's fresh air. Do you think I can do it?"

"Why wouldn't I? I've seen how you manage Pine Breeze. It's no stretch to believe you can build and run an inn." Most boys didn't seem interested in discussing their futures with me. Daddy and Mr. Bergen were too happy to discuss the new resort plans without any input from the rest of us. Thomas cared about my opinion.

He laughed. "I meant, do you believe I can afford it?"

"Thomas, you've been honest with me. Why would I doubt your funds? Is it because you can hardly believe it yourself?"

"Yes, I think you've hit the nail on the head." He turned on his side to face me. "I think I brought you out here to prove to someone that I'm building a future. Someone who can keep my secret and believes in me."

"I believe in you. But I also think you brought me out here to kiss me again." I tilted my head. "Did you?"

"Come here, Caitrin." He reached out and pulled my face to his.

The exhilaration didn't diminish even though this wasn't our first kiss. In fact, if anything the flutters in my belly were bigger now.

Lying alongside him, my breath coming in pants. I allowed my hands to roam over his arms, and I used a finger to outline his collarbone.

"Can I unbutton your shirt?" I asked even as I started on the top button.

He nodded and watched my shaking fingers as I opened

his shirt. He removed it along with his undershirt and lay back down beside me. I had never been so close to a man's skin before. He didn't move as I felt the planes of his body. His skin was pale, indicating he never sunbathed as the guests did. His heartbeat thumped against his chest as I bent to kiss it.

A guttural moan issued from his throat as he rolled over, so that I lay on my back. He was careful to keep his right hand tucked behind him.

"May I?" His left hand was poised at the hem of my sweater.

I nodded so eagerly, I bumped my head against the hard ground.

He chuckled and slid his hand under my top. His fingers played on the edge of my bra and I arched into them, my body craving more than the achingly light touches he gave. I didn't care if I seemed loose. I didn't want to regret a moment.

Shoving the elastic of my bra, he filled his left hand with my breast. The electricity that went through my blood sent my heart to palpitations.

"Please more," I moaned just like a wanton woman in those novels Marilyn hid under her bed. I fumbled behind and unhooked my bra in the back offering myself to him.

"You don't want me touching you." His gravelly tone broke my trance and I glanced to his right hand he kept at his side.

"I do," I demanded, pulling my top completely off so I was as nude as him. I took his right wrist and pulled it to my chest.

The air didn't cool my blood, even if it did send prickles along my skin. And sure enough, he used both hands to caress me. I didn't notice his missing fingers, because he had started using his mouth on my nipple. Flicks of his tongue spread wet heat across my skin.

"Oh." I had no idea that was part of lovemaking. Maybe it was something only Irish people did. None of the girls who had been with boys had ever mentioned it to me. But then, they had only experienced sex in the back of cars, never on the dewy grass of the most beautiful spot in the Catskills.

He moaned against my chest, causing even more vibrations to ring in my blood.

He settled his left hand on the front of my trousers. "I'm going to touch you, but keep your clothes on."

I tried to respond that I could undo my pants, but I heard my gasp ring out in the trees as the pressure from his fingers through my clothes shot pulses through my core.

My hips rocked on their own, knowing instinctively what a woman should do with a man. My body seemed to strain against itself, as the pressure increased. Only in the quiet privacy of my room had I known this feeling. But with Thomas, the mounting tightness was magnified. His fingers' pace grew frantic as my head thrashed from side to side.

I didn't want to remove my hands from gripping his strong back. But this was my opportunity. With tentative touches, I found the outline of his member, full and strong, underneath the fly of his trousers. I was desperate to explore its shape, even as his fingers continued their rhythmic work between my legs.

Abruptly he pulled his hand away. My body screamed in protest.

"Caitrin, my love. I can't go further," he whispered in my ear.

"Yes, further. I want to know what it means to be a woman. Take me, Thomas. Please." I tried to sound sure and confident, instead of weak and pleading.

"No, not here. And not…" He rolled off me and stared at the now blue-tinged sky. "I can't offer you what a man should offer you if he's going to take your virginity."

"I don't want anything from you. I mean, I don't expect anything from you." I touched his glistening skin, hot from exerting control.

"But I expect better from myself." He turned to look at me, and if I were a more experienced woman I would have been able to tell what his serious expression meant. "Let's get dressed."

Wordlessly, we dressed and walked to the boat.

"Please don't think I'm a loose charity girl, knoddling with every boy." I kept my gaze on the boathouse, which was growing larger as we approached, the oars making tiny splashes as he rowed.

"I'd never think anything like that. You're a good girl, Caitrin. You're brave and smart. I don't want you to regret an action done from boredom or in rebellion against your father's tight rein."

"Thank you. You're honorable." Which only made me

like him more. "I need to do something adventurous or I'll crawl out of my skin."

"Don't be doing that, it's such pretty skin." His smile was infectious. "Keep your ear to the ground, Caitrin. You'll find your opening. When you do, pounce. Don't let anyone pinch a chance away. If I can buy a corner of land then save for the building costs, then you'll make your dream come true. It's not always the obvious path, but when it presents itself, you'll know."

"You're not like other boys. You care about what I want." Adventure was still my goal, but Thomas's consideration made me think about more than simple adventure. The long future came after any brief thrilling moment.

We slipped into the boathouse and the first few early birds were staking their spots on the beach. I helped stow the oars and when Thomas put the boat away an unfamiliar awkwardness came between us.

"This isn't good-bye, is it?" I asked.

"I think your family is booked for another week." He stared into my eyes, but it was my heart that felt the gaze.

"You know what I mean." I placed my hand on his forearm, the sinews rippling beneath my touch.

"What good can come of it?" He brushed a few strands of my hair already bursting from the pins.

"I want to see you again. Spend time before I have to leave."

"It's almost more painful than not seeing you again at all."

"Thomas." I fell into his chest, his heartbeat a drum tolling the end.

He kissed the top of my head, gently pushed me back, and slid outside.

I waited a few moments so we wouldn't be seen leaving together. Then forced a casual pace in the steps I took toward the dining room. A story of an early morning walk formed in my mind that would explain my showing up to breakfast from the beach and not my room. I might have to make excuses to my family, but I felt no shame in what I did.

The only shame I would ever feel where Thomas Cullen was concerned was not noticing that he could be much more than a summer fling. Blinded by anger, I'd looked to do something rash. But his wise words about looking for opportunity gave me hope for my own future and maybe one with a man who wanted me to have my own future.

Chapter 6

THOMAS

With Bergen feeling anxious about getting staff for the Belvedere, he sent me on a headhunting mission. Combining that with my day off, I could spend a blissful three days among my people. And leaving Pine Breeze for a few days might cool things off with Caitrin after our too-hot boat ride.

"Well, Tommy Cullen, the big shot from over the hill graces us with his presence." Martin Finnegan winked and pulled me a pint before I was even seated. He was the owner, manager, barkeep, social director (which meant he hung up a dartboard), and sometimes cook (when his wife was busy) for the Glagorm Resort on the Irish side of the Catskills.

Here I could be "Tommy." My manhood wasn't at risk, because the people who knew me as a pain-in-the-neck young lad never saw me as a man. And it was refreshing to be cared for.

I took a long swallow. "That's delightful. It's going to be good to have the lot of you waiting on me for a few days. Speaking of which." I reached into my jacket pocket for my wallet. "I want to pay you for the room I know Mary set aside for me. She said I couldn't stay in the staff rooms as they're full."

"Your money is no good here." Martin stacked glasses without looking up.

"And your modesty is no good with me. I won't rack up debt with you. I owe you already for giving me that job years ago."

"You owe me nothing but kindness. Don't insult me with your money. And you can earn your keep by placating Old Seamus. He was grumbling about the pipes and laying aside some wrenches with your name on them."

I nodded, finished downing my beer, and stood. "What whiskey will not cure, there is no cure for. I'll go meet my fate with the pipes. Can I stow my bag behind your fair bar until I've worked for my keep?"

Martin took my bag and tucked it behind his clean bar. I strode toward the shed where I was confident I'd find Seamus McGillins, the man who'd saved my soul, if not my life.

The tinkering of metal greeted me as I approached the familiar workspace. In the immediate years after I lost my father, and a good portion of my fingers, hopelessness had overtaken me. Seamus had taken me under his wing, showed me how to keep Glagorm Resort running, if not smoothly, then at least well enough so no one noticed the aging plumbing. He also showed me I had a home, and some sort of family.

"You just going to stand there with your teeth in your mouth, or are you going to come help an old man?" Seamus didn't turn around but continued to hammer at a stubborn connector.

"I don't see any old men." I came alongside him, fitting next to him at the workbench as naturally as if I hadn't left seven years ago.

"You can work on separating out that bit of busted pipe. We've got to save all the good pieces we can. Still can't get any new materials. The war machine has stopped but those company bosses haven't opened up shop to the rest of us yet."

"How is the season here?"

He shrugged. "GIs came back, wanted to drink away what they had seen, and fuck new memories. I wouldn't be surprised if there's a rush of weddings in the next few months."

"Love is blooming." I wrestled with the busted end of a pipe, trying to free it from the good part it was joined to. A task made more difficult because I had to use my armpit to hold one end. Not that Seamus would offer to help.

"That would be a lot easier if you take off that fancy tuxedo you're wearing."

I put down the pipes and slid my jacket off. "It's a suit jacket. I wouldn't waste the threads of my good tux at this place."

He didn't respond but went to work on a door handle that needed tightening.

"Besides," I went on undeterred because I knew he was truly interested in my life and work. "Now that I'm going to be manager of a real high-end place, I'll need even more suits. In fact, the people paying top dollar next season expect to see me in full tails. You'd actually be impressed with the plumbing that's going in. And there's telephones in all the cottages."

Still no response came from Seamus.

"And we're installing single-handled faucets."

That got his attention. He put down his tools. "No more scalded hands, eh? Well there's nothing too fine for the swells."

"Those swells are going to be paying me enough to own my bit of land outright. No bank mortgage for me." I grunted and clenched my arm tighter around one end of the pipe.

"That your land already?"

"Almost. Garrett is trying to line up the deal."

"Ooh that Garrett Laron. He's one I wouldn't turn my back on. You watch yourself."

"See, I knew you cared about me. I'll need your help when I've got my own place built. I'll need a top-notch building engineer."

"If I live to see the day you're the boss, you can be my boss."

"It will only be a few years from now. You planning on kicking the bucket anytime soon?"

"Death is the poor man's doctor."

I rolled my eyes, gave one last tug, and the old pipe came loose.

"Here you go. I'm going to find my room. Eat some of Mary's stew and rest my feet."

"That's the first bit of hard work you've done all year."

Seamus pointed to the pipes. "Go rest your soft feet and skinny legs."

I patted his shoulder as I turned to go. The muggy air hung heavy with the end of summer humidity, so I carried my jacket over my arm. Mary, Martin's wife, had set out clean linens in a guest room closest to the dining room. I was pretty sure they were at full capacity and giving up a room for me was a generous offer considering. An offer that still made me squirm with the scorecard I kept in my mind. I'd have to do much more than help Seamus with one pipe to deserve it.

After unpacking, I sauntered into the dining room. Wood panel darkened the room, with brass fixtures giving off just enough light to find a comfortable chair. All the tables were large enough to accommodate ten people, but no two tables were the same shape. And few of the chairs matched. Heavily polished wood without tablecloths was the easel that Mary would fill with potato rolls, beef stew, and cabbage.

I didn't recognize any faces, but that didn't matter; everyone sat together.

"Tommy, sit here next to my niece Aileen. She's visiting from Chicago."

"Nice to meet you, Aileen." I took the seat between her and the husband of a newlywed couple. Even though the place was hopping and all the tables would be full, the staff would be eating with the guests tonight. That wasn't unusual on this side of the mountains. Rarely was there much differentiation between the workers and the guests.

"Aunt Mary said you manage one of the luxury Jewish resorts." Aileen's bright blue eyes were surrounded by thick dark lashes. Her black hair fell to her shoulders in waves. On another night, I might be interested in Aileen. But Mary made the stakes too high by pointedly letting me know she was her kin, and any attention would be taken too seriously by Mary and Martin.

"I do, and lovely people they are. I'm fortunate to have the work." Out of politeness, I asked about her travels from Chicago and we made small talk as the serving dishes were scraped clean.

I kept a distant but interested tone to the conversation and made sure to give attention to the other diners. This provoked a stern glance from Mary. A charming grin from me did nothing to soften her disappointment.

As Aileen helped Mary clear the dishes, the fiddlers tuned up, and the dancing started. The Wedding Jig was played in honor of the newlyweds. Tune after tune, the clogging and spinning gave the air a heady quality. Smiling was second nature when dancing along with two fiddles, a banjo, and a room of happy people. With me taking turns with everyone, I worked up quite a thirst.

I fell into my chair and lifted my glass.

"You didn't take to Aileen?" Martin was at my elbow.

"Not taking to anyone at the moment. Once I'm settled with my own business, I'll get myself taken."

"Hmmm. Aileen's father owns a nice business in Chicago. You'd be set up."

"Chicago is not the Catskills. And Aileen's father's

business is not my own."

"How's your mother?"

"Well. Her last letter told me that Maggie is excelling in school."

He nodded and stared at the dancers. "You're not here to poach my workers?"

"Just for the off season. I need hands to get the place up and running."

He nodded and drank down the last drop of whiskey from his glass. "You know I have nothing against the Hebrew people. But you'd be well set in Chicago." He pointed to Aileen. "No struggling to buy that property you're going on about. No scrimping to send money back home. You'd be among us." He waved his arms.

"If you've got nothing against the Hebrew people, why would I need to be in Chicago among the Irish?"

"I'm just saying you're taking the hard road, when an easy one is presenting itself. If you don't like Chicago, come back and work for me."

"Sometimes the hard way has the best rewards. Don't worry about me, Martin. I'm doing just fine. Besides, I like the people I work with. They're good people."

"I know. I know. But don't you want to bring Maggie and your mother back?"

"Maggie needs an education. I can't afford to keep them here and let her stay in school. She'll be able to go to university and study languages."

"She won't need schooling if you're working for Aileen's father."

I could've tried to convince Martin that I knew what was best. I could've defended my decisions. But in truth, I didn't need Martin to agree or understand. Education was what made the poor no longer poor. I didn't want my sister to depend upon a man the way my mother had. Da's death had left her penniless and helpless. With only being able to take in wash or earn a few cents cleaning houses, there was no way she could keep Maggie from working. All those widows created by the war were now having to fend for themselves. Most people wouldn't agree with me that a woman should be able to feed herself. But the world was an unpredictable and dangerous place. And I would do what I could to set Maggie up.

It didn't take long for my mind to summon up the smartest, most independent woman I had met in recent months. Most likely because Caitrin Gold was never far from my mind. A woman with her own plans, the flame of determination. Someone who was striving for more than what she was given, that was her allure. The way her body reacted to my touch also drew me to her. These few days away might give her the chance to spot someone who could be a better match. It might give me the distance to come to my senses.

Or it might make me more willing to take the risk of being near her flame.

***

CATHY

After a day spent daydreaming about our few stolen minutes on Thomas's land, I had no desire for company or dinner. I had thought of it as Thomas's land. I could picture him welcoming guests to his inn, and a young bride at his side. Yes, I did see myself as that young bride, but I knew that could never be. It wasn't only our different backgrounds. My father would plotz if I said I wanted to marry someone who wasn't Jewish. Not sure Mom would be too keen either. Besides destroying my relationship with my family, being with Thomas in the Catskills would mean completely abandoning my dream. Sure, I loved the Catskills more than anywhere else, but all the good jobs were in the grimy gritty city. I hadn't yet given up all hope of a career and independence. So, I quickly decided that Thomas would likely remain a bachelor, because that suited my fantasy.

Marilyn and I washed and dressed in simple skirts and blouses. We met Mom, Daddy, and David in the main dining room. Marilyn and David acted like they hadn't seen each other in years, when it was really only a few days that David went back home to finalize the purchase of their home. And of course, that's all we talked about. What furniture would they need? Could Marilyn please have Grandma's china? And maybe they should wait until after the wedding to buy anything to see what they got in gifts. And then Marilyn and David decided a walk instead of dessert would be nice. Which meant they were going to go smooch. But we all pretended they were getting some fresh air.

"You've been off in your own world all day. Are you still brooding?" Dad observed. Most likely because he was as fascinated by the discussion of drapes as I was.

"Daddy, you have to understand how disappointed I

am." And with vacation almost over, my fate of deadly boredom in suburban Long Island approached.

He held up a hand. "I do understand. Your mother talked my ear off last night explaining to me that if we have a daughter as brilliant as you are, then we need to find a way for you to exercise that mind."

I looked back and forth between my parents. Mom's beaming smile gave me some hope. "Really? You mean it? I can get my job back?"

"Now just hold your horses. Ah, here comes Bergen. I'll let him explain."

My confused thoughts were mirrored on Mom's face, which had fallen from her previous joy. "I thought you said you were going to talk to someone in the New York insurance office?" Mom's hushed tone was reserved for when she was truly angry.

"My favorite family. How are the Golds?" Mr. Bergen pulled up a chair and sat to join us.

"This is perfect timing. Why don't you tell Cathy the good news?" Daddy clasped his hands and rested them on the white tablecloth with a satisfied grin.

"Cathy, your father didn't need to tell me what a bright young woman you are. I've known you my entire life and I am in need of a bookkeeper for the Belvedere. I don't want you to feel that I'm doing you, or your father, a favor. It would be you doing me the favor. I need someone smart who I can trust. Someone who's like family." He leaned back in his chair, his arms expanded so that he nearly caught a rushing busboy with a tray heaped with dirty dishes.

"You want me to work as a bookkeeper? Adding accounts and…and keeping ledgers?"

"Cathy." Dad's voice was part scolding, part warning. "This is a great opportunity for you."

"I'm not ungrateful, Mr. Bergen. Just surprised." The din of the room overwhelmed me. Typically, I could block out the chatter and clatter of the enormous dining room. But my head rattled like a subway car.

"This is the perfect solution." Daddy patted Mom's hand. "She'll be completely safe and looked after here. And it's only until the Belvedere opens. Right?"

"We talked about the insurance company and her living at home." Mom's whisper was hardly quiet.

Mr. Bergen waved his arm. "Of course, once we're up and running I'll hire a real bookkeeper."

I guess a summa cum laude graduate who can calculate sums up to six digits in her head couldn't be a real bookkeeper. Heat flamed my face. The urge to sweep the glassware off the table and storm out almost overtook me.

"Who will be here?" Mom asked.

"My boy, Ron, for one. He's assistant manager of the Belvedere, and one day he'll take over the business from me. He's got quite a future."

I didn't miss Mr. Bergen's unsubtle wink toward my father. Obviously, they were hoping the "almost like family" would become "family."

"And you'll be such a good influence on my boy. He has a natural head for business, but hasn't studied as much as you have."

"Yes, I know Ron. He does have natural talents." Like menacing girls with spiders and putting salt in everyone's lemonade. But I supposed he'd grown out of that.

"See?" Daddy said to Mom. "She'll be a good influence on Ron."

"And who *else* will be here?" Mom's suspicions hadn't been alleviated.

"Thomas Cullen is my manager, and he's right now gathering staff. Borrowing some from neighboring places for the off season. He knows all the locals."

So that's why I hadn't seen him all day despite my searching every area of the resort.

"Thomas Cullen, the one who brought us cake?" Mom's voice grew even less audible.

"What New York insurance company?" I asked.

"I had thought to call someone I know. But when I asked Bergen to use the phone and explained my purpose, he had this even better plan." Daddy beamed.

Mom's eyes filled with tears as she turned to me. "You don't have to take this job," she said.

"I didn't train as a bookkeeper. The math I can do, it's way beyond this." My words were loud enough to catch the attention of the yentas at the next table. I stood, ready to walk out.

"Cathy, Mr. Bergen is making a very generous offer." He held my hand to keep me there. I used to love walking with Daddy and holding hands. We had been so in tune with each other. We both liked the same things, walks in the woods, or even walks in Central Park. I was the one he took to see the Westerns that Marilyn and Beth hated. My years at college didn't change me that much. He could no longer see me for me.

"Mr. Bergen's going to look after you and give you a position. I can't see how you can refuse." Daddy brought my attention back to the table and the three expectant faces. One hoping I could inject some brains into his son. One expecting me to fall over in gratitude for what he saw as the best chance I could get. And one worried about her daughter living on her own with a cake-bearing Irishman.

If Daddy couldn't see the real me, I would have to pretend to be the daughter he thought I was, at least until I could find another way.

"You're right, Daddy. Mr. Bergen, I'm sorry I hesitated. It's such a kind offer, and I truly am grateful. This is a great opportunity for me." I leaned over and pecked him on the cheek and repeated the process for Daddy. Then politely retook my seat and gently placed my napkin back in my lap. "I saw chocolate mousse for dessert."

"That was always one of your favorites," Daddy said.

Mom's strained expression told me she wasn't completely onboard with this plan and would have some words for Daddy later. This was the best chance I was likely to get. It was saving me from living with Mom and Daddy, and maybe Will would find someone else in the next ten months. In any case, I'd get to spend time with Thomas. Most importantly, I'd have the freedom to plan my next move.

Chapter 7

THOMAS

I took a few deep breaths and kept my clenched fists inside my pants pockets.

"So, Ronald. You'll want to make sure that at least four maids are on schedule Sunday. Guests generally leave on Sundays and we need to get those rooms cleaned." The smile on my face would never pass as friendly. But my true inner nature at that moment was too dark to be represented.

"Oh, right, you did mention that." Ron sat at his desk, in his "office," which had been a storage closet for the engineer. And I stood dutifully behind his right shoulder keeping my impatience at bay. "It's a lot to keep track of."

"It truly is. I'm sure you'll get the hang of it. Why, you've only been at it for two days." I stepped back and came around to the front of his desk, hands clasped behind my back like an attentive soldier. "I suppose you can ask some of the kitchen staff to help with the room cleaning, now that the maids have all trotted off to town." I tried to keep my tone as a question even though I had the authority to order him to do it.

"Won't that make them angry?"

"Most likely. The manager isn't always the most popular or well-liked person."

"Maybe you could ask them. They know you better. And everyone already likes you. They all say so." His pathetic attempt to butter me up didn't fool me. "And we don't need to tell the old man, do we? I mean it's not like you're doing my job for me. You are in charge of the staff."

I had wondered how long it would take the weasel to play his cards. The cards that fortune—a rich father and dead older brother—had dealt him.

"Of course. I'll talk to them right away." Because the staff did respect me, and I could soften the blow with the promise of bonus pay and an extra day off.

He sheepishly handed me the schedule, and I took it with immense flourish and deference, turned softly, and strode out.

Saints preserve us. I didn't want to have to drown Ronald Bergen in beautiful Liberty Lake.

This experiment of his father's, to give Ron a few "responsibilities" now as training, was going to end in disaster. The season was winding down and I couldn't see Ron achieving any great learning. Unless learning how to use his position was the goal.

I rushed through the kitchen inspection and carefully worded my "request" that they help in the rooms. All the while, I felt the edge of the latest letter from my mother in my pocket. I had read it already, but wanted to savor it once more.

Pride swelled in my chest when I pictured little Maggie speaking French like a true Parisian. And she had even started on German. The opportunities available for a young woman who could translate were endless. With Europe mixing together like never before, they would need swarms of translators and Mags was just the person to do it. She could escape the dreary Irish land. The poverty and deprivation. For all its lush greenery, nothing grew on that rock but sadness. She would earn her own way, or even meet some diplomat and have an easy life. All the dollars not saved toward my land on the lake were not going to waste. It might take that much longer to start my dream, but I wouldn't forsake my family.

"You're lost in your own world." The melody of Caitrin's voice pulled me up from my wandering through the playing fields.

"Well, hello, Caitrin. I was, indeed, lost in thought. What brings you out to the playing fields when there aren't any games scheduled?"

"I was looking for you." Her coy mouth grinned, and the memory of the taste of those lips sent a shudder through my veins.

"You've found me." I spread my arms out and she laughed. "Care to walk with me to the beach as I find an unwitting staff member to berate for not having enough towels available?"

"Sounds lovely." She fell into step beside me but did not loop her arm through mine. She sensed, as I did, any touch would be dangerous. A small ember could ignite a blazing wildfire. "Your face was so deep in thought, I could tell you were a million miles away." Her voice held a curious, innocent tone.

"Not so far as that. Merely across the ocean. My mother wrote to me about my little sister. Her studies in languages are going very well, and she's likely to get a job in Europe translating."

"You're very proud of her."

"I couldn't be happier. It was a hard decision to send them back to Ireland, especially during the war. But I couldn't keep them here without my sister going into service, and I wanted her to have an education."

"You should be proud of yourself, then as well."

"All I do is send the money. But you were looking for me. What's on your mind?"

"I have big news, Thomas. Where can we go so I can tell you in private?"

"Come this way." I took a small step ahead of her so we could proceed single file to the shed outside of the offices. "No one comes here in the middle of the day. It holds extra chairs and supplies for the dining room if we're having a big event." I unlocked the shed and stepped into the musty space.

With just enough room for two small inches to separate our faces, I sensed her excitement.

"You're nearly vibrating with urgency. What is this big news?"

"I've got a job. Not the kind I originally wanted. But I think you're going to be very happy."

"Caitrin, that's wonderful. Of course, I'm happy for you."

Before I knew it, her lips were on mine. I shouldn't

have accepted her kiss. But she offered and I was weak, made of flesh like any man.

"You might be happy for yourself, too." She bounced on her toes, and I desperately tried not to look at the contour of her lacy bra through the sheer chiffon blouse as she did.

"Well, tell us the rest." I placed my hands on her slim shoulders, feeling her softness beneath my palms.

"I'll be working for you. At the Belvedere. Meet your new bookkeeper." She thrust out her hand for a handshake, but the lack of space meant her fingers grazed my midsection.

I dropped my hands and they fell useless to my sides. "You're working here?"

"Aren't you pleased? We'll get to spend more time together."

"That's exactly what I'm not pleased about. Caitrin, you can't work as a bookkeeper for Bergen."

"Why not? You don't think I can do the work." Spots of anger rose in her pale face.

"You could do the work of a thousand men. You could keep the books in your sleep. That's not the problem. We—we can't work together."

"Nonsense. You'll treat me fairly. I know you'll be a good boss."

"Caitrin. The only way I am able to be around you is because I know you'll be gone soon. In a matter of days, your family is due to depart and I was never going to see you again. The feelings we have for each other have to fade over time. That can't happen if you're working under me." The double meaning lost on the beautiful young girl only made me wince.

"Thomas, why do the feelings have to fade? Why can't we see where they lead?'

"I know where they lead, and they lead to nowhere good. For either of us. For my future, for your future."

"You were the one who told me to be on the lookout for my opportunity. Well, this is my opportunity. I'm not passing it up."

"How can your father agree to this?"

"Mr. Bergen is like an uncle to me. The only reason Daddy agreed to let me take the job in the first place is because he thinks I'll be safer here, under Mr. Bergen's care, than by myself at some boarding house. Besides, who do I need protecting from?"

"Me." My voice was husky with desire, anger, and confusion.

Her body stiffened for the first time since I'd known her. A chill from the lake blew into the shed.

"You'll have to cope with your future somehow, because this is my future. I am working at the new resort as a bookkeeper. I'm escaping my parents' house. I'm escaping marriage to Will. And you can't stop me." Her exit wasn't as dramatic as she probably had hoped for, as a few stray boxes prevented her from storming out in one motion.

I stayed in the shed for a moment to catch my breath. My chest constricted as if I had run miles. That's what being in Caitrin Gold's presence did to me. Both when she was soft and supple under my hands, and when her icy temper flared between us.

I left the shed, locked it behind me, and glanced at the open window immediately to my left.

Damn my stupid woman-addled brain.

That storage room turned office for dimwit Ron was directly next to the shed. A soft scraping of a chair against the rough floor let me know someone was in there.

What he heard or didn't hear couldn't concern me at that moment. Luncheon was due to start any minute. And the comedy acts scheduled that evening had called to say the car they were using to leave the city had broken down.

Starting the new resort for Mr. Bergen was going to be the final feather in my cap before I saved enough to open my own place. My crowning last achievement that would launch me to my own business. Now, saddled with an idiot assistant manager and an alluring bookkeeper, I could only pray that my current job didn't end before my future even started.

***

CATHY

Thomas's words stung. To be honest, I did understand his point of view. In his mind, I was a simple innocent girl who had no idea what she was getting herself into. He saw himself as more of a danger to me than I knew he could be. Because even if he "ruined my virtue" it didn't matter. My virtue wasn't something I was overly concerned with.

My best move was to stay away, allow Thomas to get used to the idea of working with me. I was sure that over time he would see that we could make a great team. And he might even agree to be my lover for a time. I could learn so much from him. Not just in business.

So for the last few days of our stay, I steered clear of Thomas Cullen. And I threw myself into resort life. Swimming, Simon Says, dancing, every darn fun thing I could do. Because after all, it was my new career.

"Cathy, why did it take you until the very end of our vacation to start enjoying yourself?" Mother shuffled the deck of cards getting ready for another round of bridge. We weren't allowed to be partners. Beth and Marilyn said we would clean the floor with them. This meant I had to endure Marilyn's endless indecision and distracted air as she pondered her hand.

"I guess it took me a while to settle in."

"I hardly have a moment here before we have to go home," Beth grumped. "Isn't there any chance I can go to farm camp?"

"Beth, you just got back from school. Everyone misses you."

"Besides, Daddy doesn't want you associating with the Commies." Marilyn arranged and rearranged her cards.

"It's not like they're Bolsheviks, they're only Socialists." Beth made her bid and chewed her fingernail until Mother swatted her hand away.

Mother placed her cards face down on the table and sighed. "I just want you girls together for a little while. With Marilyn getting married and Cathy spending the year up here, I won't have my girls around me much longer."

The excitement about my new job waned as I pictured Mom alone in the house. Daddy at work, Marilyn setting up her own home. Beth back at school, and me off on my career adventure.

"Sorry, Mom. I don't want you to be lonely." I leaned over to peck her cheek. I was on the verge of encouraging her to get out to do something. Volunteer work, work at the synagogue. But she already did all those things and it wasn't enough to occupy her mind.

"Having an empty nest is better than the alternative. Having children who can't take care of themselves," she said under her breath as Ron Bergen entered the library.

"If it isn't all the beautiful Gold girls." His smile was as wide as his father's. But he wouldn't age as well as his dad had. Already, his face was soft from some extra weight and his shoulders slightly stooped.

"Hello, Ron. It's so good to see you. I thought your limbo contest was a great success." Mom had a way of sounding sincere when I knew she thought limbo was a ridiculous game, and the fact that three older men had sprained something in the process was a disaster.

"I knew we needed to add a little something *nouveau* to our *repertoire*." His emphasis on the last word only showed his ignorance instead of his cleverness.

"You did study French in anticipation you'd be sent there, didn't you?" Mother's tinkling laugh almost made me choke.

"One doesn't need to go overseas to develop a refined taste. I've been traveling around the US staying at fine hotels.

All to help in setting up the Belvedere, of course."

"Of course." Mom nodded in a placating way the childish Ron couldn't grasp.

"My father's given me a great job there. It's assistant manager, but really I'll be in charge of most of the setup. And I'll be earning a good salary, probably as much as the regular manager. Cathy will be a great asset for us. Mrs. Gold, you can be assured I'll look after her."

"She's very much looking forward to starting her duties." Mom looked at me with the expression that said I needed to chime in.

"Yes, I am so grateful to you and your father." I tried out a smile, showing my teeth and all. Mom kicked me under the table. I raised my voice a few octaves. "This is exactly the type of job I was looking for. And it's just like working with family. You're like the *brother* I never had."

Marilyn coughed and Beth covered her mouth to hide her smirk.

Ron's pudgy face bloomed a bit pink; he excused himself with some vague explanation of having to see to something and strode out.

"I have no idea why you want to work with him." Beth shook her head.

"I don't think it's Ron she wants to work with," Marilyn muttered under her breath.

Mom shot a warning glare at Marilyn. I'm sure Mom had guessed at my interest in Thomas. She wasn't dim-witted. But she recognized my desperation to do any kind of work other than as Daddy's secretary or Will's wife. I could be more than she ever dreamed. Well, maybe she did dream it. She just couldn't make it happen.

"Whose turn is it? I've lost concentration." I tossed my cards on the table.

Beth scooped them and shuffled.

"Thanks, Mom. For allowing me to take this job. I know it's a burden to you and a risk."

She waved her hand. "You each need to follow your own path. I support you girls. You only have one youth. Don't spend it doing what everyone expects you to do."

"Does that mean I can go to farm camp?" Beth looked up from her game of solitaire.

"I draw the line at *kibutz* farm camp. Spend a few weeks with your family before you shoot off back to boarding school. Who knows what you get up to with the Socialists?"

***

THOMAS

The weather hadn't yet turned cool, and the last holdouts dotted the shore of the lake. A few stray families always took advantage of the September sunshine. The tips of the maple leaves turned from their lush green to a canary yellow on their way to a blood red.

The bird songs were still just as loud, but more prominent as the crowds had dispersed. The majority of the staff had migrated away as well. Back to college for the waiters and other young people. Down south to pick the crops for the groundskeepers. And back to Manhattan for most of our cooks. People returned to New York as the cooler temperatures made city life tolerable. Not that there weren't people who tolerated the heat and stench all year. But for those with bank accounts big enough to accommodate an escape from the garbage that cooked in the streets during August, they could safely return to New York, choosing to take no notice of those who stayed to keep their precious city running.

"Mr. Cullen, what should we do about luncheon? We've got spaghetti, sardines, and roast chicken. Hardly things that go together." Ethel Nussbaum approached me just outside the kitchen.

"Toss some salad and put out all the cookies. It almost doesn't matter what we serve, just serve large portions. We've got to move everything out."

"I'll let everyone know. And, Mr. Cullen, I was wondering if I might stay here a bit longer. My sister says her extra room won't be ready for me for a few weeks yet, and I guess I could stay at a rooming house until she's ready for me."

"Stop talking nonsense, Mrs. Nussbaum." I kept my tone even but wouldn't condescend to her. She deserved respect. "You know very well that someone has to stay and cook for me and the workmen building the new resort. Mr. Ron Bergen will be here as will Catherine Gold. I'll need a small staff to help set up the place. I hope you're not thinking of quitting."

Her eyes lit up and a youthful flush colored her cheeks. "You know I'm able to do anything you ask of me."

"You're a loyal and hard worker. We're lucky you are able to stay on throughout the year. I hope your sister won't be too disappointed to lose your company."

"I think she'll manage without me. She might need me to visit a few times over the holidays to help out, of course."

"I think we can spare you a few days here and there. But only just." I worked to keep my face straight. Ethel had her dignity and I would not take that away from her.

"Cullen." Mr. Bergen's voice boomed from the main lobby.

I briskly took my place with him. "Sir, are we ready to take a look the construction?"

"My driver is waiting if you can be spared for a while here."

"There's an international buffet planned for luncheon. Let's see how things have progressed."

We sat in silence as the large car jounced along the as-yet-unpaved road. Mr. Bergen gripped the side of seat to steady himself. His jaw set tight either against the assault to our bottoms or in concentration of the huge plans ahead.

I sucked in a breath as we crested the hill. The workmen had been busy these last few blazing hot weeks. The cottages seemed almost livable. The main structure still had a lot of work to be done. Just a skeleton was there, but the concrete had been poured for the indoor pool, and the footprint of the entertainment hall was clearly outlined.

"Leaves me speechless, too." Bergen heaved himself out of the car and we stood side by side, admiring the wonder of what man could build.

"It is just as impressive as a skyscraper," I said.

"I think it's prettier." Bergen led the way. As we

approached the worksite, the noise of the crew and their machinery grew.

My heartbeat echoed the hammers. The hum of insects was replaced by the hum of human accomplishment. It was difficult to not be impressed by the scope of this endeavor.

"I compliment your vision, sir. This is truly a remarkable project."

"And you're at the front of it, son. Let's hope that nothing comes in the way."

I was about to ask what his concerns were, when he conferred with the foreman who assured us that the project was on schedule. All outside work would be done by November, allowing the crew to move indoors, finishing the electrical work and painting, when the weather turned cold.

"And how soon can my staff move in? I want them on the grounds as they prepare for Memorial Day weekend." Bergen said the date with such flourish, it might have been V-E Day.

"If they're none too finicky about reading at night, a few cottages will be ready at the end of September. They should choose the ones with fireplaces. Not like these quarters are quite fit for winter living. But they'll be good enough."

"Do you think you and the staff can handle it? A little discomfort builds character, doesn't it, Thomas?"

"Of course." Although, I wondered how much more character Ethel Nussbaum needed. I certainly felt developed enough that I'd like to be able to not freeze to death in my bed come January. But a fire in the hearth together with a fire in the belly would keep me warm. I certainly wouldn't ask Bergen for any favors. What he offered is what I would take and not a scrap more. Let him think he owed me for putting up with these conditions.

An image flashed through my brain of Caitrin Gold huddled by a fire, her cheeks flushed, her hair cascading down her nightdress. That would not be the way for me to keep warm.

I'd done my best to ignore the fact that she would be showing up again soon. In only a few weeks, I'd have to pick her up at the train station, her many cases of luggage filled with impractical items, and her damned competence, which I probably needed but didn't want to admit to needing.

"So as soon as the last hangers-on depart Pine Breeze, you and whoever is left will choose some cottages to move into. Mind you take care of them well. It's the last time the staff will be sleeping in accommodations such as these."

"We'll be mindful of the honor. Speaking of which, Mr. Bergen. Although the structures are grand and fit to be lived in, we don't as yet have beds."

He snapped his fingers. "Darn it all. That's why I rely on you. Can we get the beds and mattresses here in time?"

"It all depends upon which beds you're interested in."

"The finest carved headboards and the plushest mattresses. Nothing less."

"If we use the furniture supplier we have in the past, they provide a good product, but of course, they won't have the volume we need right now."

"You'll figure something out. You always do."

He strode off to survey the rest of the buildings, and I was left to figure something out.

Chapter 8

CATHY

Typically, the whirlwind of planning a wedding would wear me thin. But the endless unimportant details of bridesmaid dress bows couldn't bother me one little bit. I didn't even mind that Mom and Marilyn had picked out a plum-colored dress for me to wear. It looked almost black, like I was mourning the loss of my own prospects.

As we walked home from Sukkot services, the crunch of leaves under our feet urged me forward. The beginning of the new Jewish year would also be a new beginning for me. Not a moment was to be wasted on silly wedding plans. Even though that's all people seemed to be able to talk about at synagogue.

"Short veils are all the fashion, Mom," Marilyn insisted as we neared our front door.

I didn't wait to hear Mom's response. She would eventually give in to everything Marilyn asked for. David would be wearing a white dinner jacket instead of a black suit. It seemed that a wedding was now more like a Hollywood gala than a sacred ceremony. Neither of which appealed to me. But I could wait. My future was so close I could taste the crisp fall apples of the Catskills.

I dashed up to my room to take inventory of what I

would bring with me. A sturdy pair of boots, all the warm sweaters I owned, terribly unattractive long johns that I was sure I would need for under my clothes, and my slide rule. There was probably very little complex computations involved. But the presence of it on my desk would bring me comfort. I'd have to wear my big winter coat, because it wouldn't fit in my trunk. Just one small trunk. I'd look like Grandma Rose getting off the boat, wearing all her clothes so she didn't have to carry much. I could bring every essential item in one trunk. No more than I would need. Unencumbered by my past.

"Why are you hiding in your room?" Mom entered and sat on my bed. "We've got a meal to prepare, and you said you'd help with the apple cake."

"Just making sure I have everything. Do we have any other wool sweaters?"

"Why don't you bring Grandma's fur? She wanted you to have it."

"I can hardly show up to work wearing sable."

"You're not a Socialist, too. Are you? Beth lectured me all the way back to school about wealth and ownership."

"Don't worry. She's going through a phase." I plopped down next to her on the bed. "I need to fit in. I want to be taken seriously for my skills."

She wrapped her arm around me and I leaned into her. The comforting smell of roses filled my nose. The soft fabric of her dress caressed my cheek.

"They'll take one look at you doing sums without paper and they'll have to take you seriously." She kissed the top of my head.

Unbidden, a few tears ran down my face. "I'm scared. I want to go, but I'm scared."

"I would hope you would be. Even when you were at college, you were never really on your own. Those housemothers kept a close eye on you. You'll be earning your own wage, making your own *decisions*." She emphasized that last word.

"*Mother*." My face already hot from crying, now flamed from embarrassment.

"I am human. And I have eyes. Thomas Cullen paid you undue attention while we were at Pine Breeze. I don't doubt that he is a good man, but he is a man. I simply don't want you to take any chances with your future. Whether that future is having a family of your own or a career. A woman's way is fragile. Not because we are, but because one misstep and any opportunity is lost."

"I promise not to ruin myself. I'm there to work, to learn about business."

"There are things you can do. Ways to prevent having a child."

"We can't talk like this. It isn't right. You shouldn't be encouraging me in that direction."

"I'm not encouraging you. But I know you. You're looking for an adventure. And you think you've found it in Thomas. But do you think he'd ever marry you? Not because you're not worthy, but you wouldn't fit into each other's worlds."

"I'm not looking to fit into his world. I just want to

work, start myself on a career, and then find someone whose world I can fit into."

"You don't get both." She paused but stared into the distance, rubbing her hand on her skirt, clearly ready to finally share her long-ago cut-off dreams.

"Both of what?" Daddy stood in the doorway to my room.

"Both her heavy woolen coat and Mama's big fur." Mother's expression magically transformed into her typical warm and relaxed demeanor.

"It's nonsense to bring that fur. There's no decent place to wear a fur in the Catskills. In fact," Daddy moved into the room and glanced into my open suitcase. "If it gets to be too much, if the work is too hard, if you're lonely, you can come home at a moment's notice. I'll drive up myself to get you."

Daddy's assurance was the best motivation for me to stay there through the bitterest conditions.

"It will be a wonderful chance for me to learn business skills."

"Business skills." Daddy laughed. "You never know. You might take to the hotel business… But even if you don't, it might come in handy. You'll be learning all about entertaining and decorating. There are always ladies looking for help with that. It could make you very popular in the temple sisterhood."

"I think Cathy has her sights higher than the Temple Beth-Am Sisterhood," Mother said with a smile. She stood from my bed and linked her arm though Daddy's. "Let's let Cathy finish arranging her belongings. And don't forget, luncheon tomorrow with David's mother and sister."

"The *machatunim*." Daddy snorted. "Glad I can skip that one. Nothing worse than spending time with the in-laws." Daddy guided Mom out, giving her a warm look and a peck on the cheek. The color rose in Mother's face and her mouth broke into a wide smile, as it always did when Daddy showed affection. She leaned in to his side as they walked downstairs for Daddy to drink coffee while Mom cooked.

Glimpses like these were proof of their love. Mom had given something up for that love. Something that hovered underneath.

I closed the lid to my trunk and shoved it under my bed. I had a week before I left, and the wedding events would take up most of my time. Sitting at my small desk, I thumbed through the bookkeeping textbook I took out from the library.

None of the topics gripped me terribly, and after reading it through once I pretty much had the subject well in hand. It gave me something to think about instead of Thomas Cullen. Thomas Cullen, the man who was going to act as if we hadn't shared the most passionate kisses. The man who insisted we couldn't work together if there was even a hint of romance.

I took a deep breath, meant to steady my heart. But the shakiness of it only reinforced what I knew. I would do my best to ignore my feelings for him. I would take on any challenge the job presented, but the bigger challenge would be denying those memories.

Chapter 9

CATHY

The train rattled to a stop, and I wrestled my case down the steps to the platform. Despite being the only passenger getting off, the conductor couldn't be bothered to help me. But an independent woman didn't need help with her luggage.

I half dragged the overstuffed case to the end of the platform where summer vacationers would typically find taxis and resort-owned vans to shuttle them to their relaxation.

I peered through the empty parking lot, a stray rusting bicycle lay on its side, and a farmer's produce truck idled at the end, letting day laborers out after a morning of picking the last of the fall crops.

An independent woman might be expected to carry her own belongings, but walking nearly five miles to her place of work seemed unreasonable.

I perched on the edge of the trunk and decided I would wait exactly thirty minutes, as I checked my watch. Then I would ask the station master to call me a taxi. Only, glancing at the ticket window, I read a sign explaining that the office was closed after one PM in winter months. October was hardly a "winter month," but I supposed that when the population of your town dropped by over a half after September, it could seem like a desolate time.

Twenty-seven minutes later, the Pine Breeze Resort van rumbled to a stop in front of me.

Thomas Cullen didn't hurry as he parked the vehicle and ambled over to where I sat, with my keister permanently indented from the case. But I'm ashamed to say that my heart was the most affected by his approach. My heart, which wouldn't listen to my head and insisted that romance could bloom with my boss.

"Have you been waiting long?"

Yes, I've been waiting twenty-seven minutes. My nose is running and I can't feel the tips of my ears.

"It's no problem. I've been enjoying the fresh country air." I was going to prove to Thomas that I was a capable woman. I would be a reliable and strong worker. And my heart could quit its yapping about his blue eyes, mischievous smile, and inner strength.

"Wonderful. Can I help you with your trunk?"

"That would be very nice, although I have managed it just fine."

"I have no doubt you have, but let me be a gentleman."

I would let Thomas Cullen be a gentleman; I would have let him do almost anything. But I had decided that if he could put up a wall between us, I could too. If he was going to pretend those kisses never happened, I was at least going to pretend to pretend they never did either.

"How was your sister's grand wedding?" he asked after we were seated in the front of the van.

"Grand is the right word. I'll say this, the Rosemere Country Club is unlikely to see another event like that anytime soon."

"Quite a lot of fuss?"

"Fuss and bother. I think about the quick ceremony, compared with the endless hours of dinner and dancing. It seems like the emphasis is on the wrong place. Even a quicker signing of the *ketubah* was rushed through."

"Signing the what?" Thomas mostly kept his eyes on the road, but when he glanced at me, I swallowed hard and gripped my hands together so as not to reach out to stroke his jaw.

"The *ketubah* is a marriage contract. It lays out the rights and responsibilities of the husband and wife."

"Sounds more like a business deal than a love affair."

"It's a wonderful thing for the bride. She gets to know that her husband is under legal obligation to care for her. He can't just toss her aside. She has some rights at least."

Thomas navigated the small road and stared out to the horizon. "Then I approve of that. I've seen too many women left with nothing." He didn't elaborate, and it didn't seem right to press him. Especially given what was nagging the back of my mind and forcing its way out.

"Thomas, we haven't spoken since you found out I'd be working here. And I want to tell you, I've been doing a lot of thinking about what you said."

"Which part was that? When I lost my temper? I apologize for speaking harshly to you."

I waved his apology away. "No, I understand why you

acted that way. I put you in a difficult situation. And I've come to agree with you. Not that I'm giving up my job. That part I don't agree with. But I can see the wisdom of keeping our distance. I want more than anything to have a career, and I'm not going to have one if I jeopardize it by having an affair."

Thomas coughed and almost ran the car off the road. After a moment, he regained control of the car and himself. "I don't remember an affair being an option."

"Don't play innocent with me, Thomas Cullen." I smiled and dug my nails into my palm to steady my voice. "We were overcome by the summer heat. Now, with the cold reality of the tasks ahead, I don't think we have feelings for each other anymore."

"We don't?" He raised a questioning eyebrow as we pulled into the dirt road to what would be the Belvedere.

"No. We will have a strictly professional relationship. Oh my." The building site was no longer a building site. Well, maybe it still was, as the workmen scurried about. But the structures were up. The main building with its elegant wraparound veranda stood among the smaller buildings—the swimming pool, the athletic facility, and the cottages, which appeared to be full-size homes.

"Yes, the work has gone very quickly. The interiors aren't complete, but you can tell she's going to be a grand place."

He pulled the car alongside some trucks where men were unloading coils of wire.

"Electricity is being hooked up in the next few days. Let

me take your things to where you'll be staying."

I followed Thomas as we picked our way carefully over the field rutted by tire tracks and loose stones.

"That's where the staff will be." He pointed toward a squat structure that bordered the woods. "They couldn't get the plumbing there in time. We're all staying in the cottages until we can move in. But don't get too comfortable. As soon as we're able to outfit the cottages, we're to move into the staff house."

"I'm fine. As long as there is a bed and place to wash up, I'm ready for work."

"Uhn-huh." Thomas walked up the steps to a cottage with "Sutherland" painted with scroll work around it.

"Sutherland?"

He put my trunk down with a thud and dug in his coat for a large ring with keys. "Mr. Bergen is naming all the cottages after European places." He searched through the keys. "He wants each one to be decorated in a different theme depending on its name." He worked a key into the lock. "Doesn't much matter to me. But dealing with Lilian Hemple, the designer, is enough to make me want to paint them all white, put in army cots, and call them finished."

He shoved open the door, and I stepped in after. An army cot and plain white walls would be an improvement.

The barren room hadn't been painted at all, and wires dangled from where fixtures would eventually go. A mattress on the unfinished floor by the hearth was the only thing that absorbed the echoes of our steps.

"This room of the cottage is the most comfortable,

because of the fireplace. The bedrooms don't have them and we can't have you freezing to death." He stood, hands on hips. "I'll have one of the men bring in a dresser for your clothes."

"Th-thank you." I swallowed and kept my hands in my coat pockets for warmth and to keep myself from shaking.

"The good news is that the fixtures in the bathroom are all installed." He led the way into the bathroom. "Of course, the water heater isn't in place yet."

"Of course." I straightened my spine.

"Listen, Cathy. I don't want to tell you what to do. But this is no place for you. It's cold and getting colder. The hours are going to be long, as the books are a mess to start with, not that it won't be a piece of cake for you to fix. I've tried to keep up best I can, but Mr. Bergen kept saying, 'Wait for Cathy Gold, she'll set it right.' And on top of his demands, there's the designer, the few staff that are here, and the incompetent Ronald Bergen I have to watch over." He took a breath and for the first time since he met me at the station, looked into my eyes with that intensity that had sent a rush through my body. "Cathy, go home. Find a job that allows you the comforts you deserve and uses the brains God gave you."

"That's quite a speech for someone who isn't going to tell me what to do." I stuck out my chin in what my mother called *the determined Cathy pose*. "I will be just fine, thank you. Warm baths are overrated. Now I think I'll freshen up and start my duties."

We stood too close in the intimate space of the

bathroom. It became painfully clear that everything I had said about not having feelings for each other was a terrible lie. But I would not budge. I would not fall the few inches forward into his chest, wrap my arms around his neck, and tilt my head back so our lips were a whisper apart.

Thomas wasn't going to let that happen either.

He nodded, turned on his heel, and strode to the door, his footfalls rattling the floorboards.

"When you're ready, you can find me in the offices. I've got everything you'll need to get started." The honey-soft tone of his voice had hardened. And now he sounded like my high school teacher, threatening to tell my parents that instead of doing the boring rote math exercises, I had been reading a chemistry journal in my lap.

Go ahead and threaten, Thomas Cullen. And don't think I didn't notice you called me Cathy.

I needed to be out of my parents' home as I needed air to breathe, and if this was the only way I could start an independent life, then so be it.

So what if I was cold. So what if the work was boring. So what if I had no one to confide in. And so what if the only light and warmth was the memories of a few stolen summer kisses.

Chapter 10

THOMAS

The devil was laughing at me for my predicament.

I sat at my desk and shuffled the papers in front of me. I couldn't read one more memorandum from the designer or Bergen. I couldn't process one more request from staff, or calculate one more bill. And I didn't have the stomach to carefully review the letter from Garrett explaining that there was still no sign I could buy that land.

Caitrin's steely-eyed glare still shot through my chest. It was all bravado; still, it was unlikely she'd give up and go home any time soon. If ever.

No, I would have to learn to work with the gorgeous strong woman. I'd have to curtail any thought other than treating her like another employee.

A bitter laugh escaped my throat as Ron walked in.

"What's funny?" Ron's curiosity and energy only extended to jokes, not as far as staff schedules or building permits.

"Just something my mother wrote in a letter. How are the electricians coming along?"

"Ok, I guess." Ron folded his arms across his chest.

"Maybe you could ask the head electrician how his work is progressing and find out if they will finish today." I forced the words through my teeth. If I opened my mouth I was liable to bite Ron's head off.

"I guess I could do that." He stood in my office still looking around.

"You might be able to do that now. If you're not too busy with other tasks." I knew very well he wasn't busy with other tasks because I assigned him so few tasks in the first place.

"Oh, sure. If there's nothing else." Ron rested his hand on the doorframe. The last thing he wanted to do was talk to the surly electrician in charge of the project. My position meant nothing to him.

My gaze darted to the desk in the corner. The desk outfitted for a bookkeeper.

"There is one more thing, Ron. Why did we put Miss Gold's desk in here with me? Isn't there another office she can use?"

"All the offices are filled." Ron recrossed his arms.

"There are two other offices besides the anteroom for the secretary when we hire her."

"Right, well, Chef Planto needs one, the one near the kitchen. And then…I took the other one."

Our stares met. Would I insist that Ron, as assistant manager, take Caitrin in his office? Or would I, as the one of us who is not the owner's son, share my space?

The image of Ronald staring at Caitrin's elegant neck as she sat with perfect posture at her desk made my skin crawl.

"That's fine then, we'll leave it as is. People have too much to do than unnecessarily move office desks."

Ron's posture relaxed, but he still made no move toward the electricians.

"Was there something else?"

"Only that I think I'm ready for more responsibility. I don't think you're giving me enough to do," he demanded. "I mean, you have so much on your plate." His attempt at soft soap didn't succeed.

It may have been the thought that Caitrin would walk in any moment, or it could have been the thought of him going to his father to complain about me. I thrust the pile of requests from the designer at him.

"The designer your father picked out has some outrageous demands. She thinks we really are on the French Riviera or in some old English village. You can be the liaison with her. Mostly it involves reminding her of the budget."

Ron snatched the papers away. "That's a perfect job for me. I'll be sure to learn about running the business that way."

I doubted that coping with one demanding decorator would qualify Ron to run the resort. When I got my land and inn, teaching Ron about business would be his father's problem. But the relief at not having to deal with him for the moment was a small release, freeing me up to deal with the bigger problems I was about to face.

And that desk in the corner was my biggest one.

***

CATHY

After a week of sorting through the books, the ledger was finally in order. I used up an entire box of pencils and almost wore a groove in my desk with my wrist. But anyone could look at the books and see that the Belvedere Resort was within budget. For now.

I hadn't realized just how much money Daddy had given Mr. Bergen. It might not be enough to impact our lives, but Daddy owned a third of the resort. Once the profits started coming in, Daddy would be rewarded for his investment. His investment also strengthened my resolve to make this resort the best it could be.

My resolve was further strengthened by having to keep my back to Thomas's constant stare. I could feel his eyes on me, watching, waiting for me to throw in the towel.

One week of cold showers, dark nights, and loneliness should have made me stronger.

It didn't. It made me sad and homesick. The only other woman in the resort was Mrs. Nussbaum. She cooked for the workmen and for us so she was busy all day. I would spend what free time she had listening to stories of when she was younger and had just met her now-deceased husband. She never spoke of the sons she lost in the war, and I never asked. Two sad souls sharing a few moments in between our work.

It didn't matter that the electricity had been hooked up days ago because the light fixtures hadn't arrived. I heard Ronald talking to someone about this, but accepted that I would have to continue to go to sleep when the sun went down, as the only lamps were in the offices.

"Well, it's all sorted out," I said and closed the ledger with a flourish. I turned my neck in order to see Thomas.

As usual, he sat at his desk, eyes on me.

"What?" He blinked.

"The accounts. I've updated all the accounts. The pay for the staff, the bills for the work crews. Everything is up to date. Tomorrow's activity can be entered right away."

"You're kidding. Those accounts were higgledy-piggledy."

"Now they're un-higgledy." I stood and stretched my back. Thomas quickly looked away.

"You've done remarkable work, and in a very short amount of time."

"Aren't you going to check?" The attention to detail Thomas gave to every nook and cranny of the Belvedere was remarkable. It wasn't just his drive to do well. His devotion to the business, to the success of something that didn't even bear his name, and the care he took with the staff was obvious. I hated to admire him for it.

"I don't need to check. I trust you."

"I guess I'll call it a night." I plucked my coat from the hook and was about to wrap it around me when Thomas appeared at my back and held it out for me. "Thank you," I whispered.

"I meant the compliment. You're a hard worker, and steadfast to endure these conditions. The staff housing will be ready in a few days and we can move in there."

"It's nice to have my work appreciated." It was the most I could say. If I said any more, all my anger would pour out. My frustration at being merely polite with him over these past days. My anger that he refused to act on what were obvious affections he had for me. He could trust me to muck around in the finances of a company he obviously cared about and relied on, but couldn't trust me to know my own heart.

"Good night then." Thomas returned to his desk and didn't give me another glance as I left.

The sun was setting earlier and earlier. I couldn't write a letter to my mother. And the only phone was in the office. Without a private moment there, I couldn't call either.

Didn't matter, I'd wash quickly and get into bed with my coat on top of the quilt I was given. I wouldn't even bother to light a fire tonight. Best just to bury my head under the covers and wait for day.

I ended up waiting for sleep, tossing and turning as my irritation at Thomas grew. I wanted to have an affair, to feel what it was like to be loved. This might be one of my few chances before spinsterhood set in. It wasn't like he had a wife he was being faithful toward. Men were impossible.

An owl's cry came close to my window. Peering through the uncurtained windows, I could see an unusual glow from the sky. I pulled my boots over heavy socks and wrapped the quilt over my nightgown, then stepped onto the porch.

A brilliant meteor shower cascaded through the sky. I tried to recollect the physics I'd studied, but decided to recall the sonnet by Shakespeare.

Not from the stars do I my judgement pluck;
And yet methinks I have astronomy,
But not to tell of good or evil luck,

Of plagues, of dearths, or seasons' quality;
Nor can I fortune to brief minutes tell,
Pointing to each his thunder, rain and wind,
Or say with princes if it shall go well,
By oft predict that I in heaven find:
But from thine eyes my knowledge I derive,
And, constant stars, in them I read such art
As "truth and beauty shall together thrive,
If from thyself to store thou wouldst convert";
Or else of thee this I prognosticate:
"Thy end is truth's and beauty's doom and date."

I couldn't predict the future from the stars either. But I could plan for my future. Truth and beauty. Career and love. If I was destined to have no family, at least I could allow myself an affair.

My chattering teeth told me it was time to go back inside, when another out-of-place glow caught my attention. It was lamplight, and it was coming from the farthest cottage from mine. Thomas's cottage.

Suddenly, the cold didn't penetrate my skin as I stalked across the field to the beacon of light.

I stomped up the front steps and knocked, but jiggled the handle before he had time to even ask who it was.

"Let me in this instant," I called.

The door was flung open and Thomas, in skivvies, was lit from the back by a roaring fire. "Caitrin, is there something wrong?"

"Yes there's something wrong. And don't Caitrin me

after a week of Cathys." I pushed past him to stand in the middle of a fully fitted-out room. "How do you have a light, and all this?" I waved my arms toward the crowded furnishings, letting the quilt fall to the ground, not caring that my nightgown and boots were all I wore.

"That's what brought you banging on my door in the middle of the night? I thought you were in trouble. I thought you were hurt."

"I am hurt. Why do you insist on testing me? On depriving me of at least a lamp. Why are you still trying to get rid of me?"

"I'm doing no such thing. The resort needs you. We would have never gotten those books in order without you. The bookkeeper who came in once a week was terribly slow and stupid."

"Then why aren't I rewarded with furniture and a measly light at night? Why do you save these things for yourself?"

"I live up here, all the time. These are *my* things. *All* of my possessions." Thomas's voice was a growl.

"Oh, yes. I guess that makes sense." Heat flamed my face, and I wasn't close enough to the fire for it to come from there.

"I'd thought about bringing you this lamp. I'd imagined you could use it to read at night. But…I couldn't bring myself to go to your cottage. I couldn't risk seeing you…like this." He pointed to my nightgown, which was aglow from the soft light of the fire.

"Thomas, why do we deny ourselves? I'm under no

illusion that you'll marry me. I understand the risks. I'm choosing to have a career instead of a family, that no man wants a wife who would never cook dinner or be home to raise children. But if I'm going to have a life of a career woman, do I need to live a life entirely without love? A little love, doled out in minutes rather than a lifetime of a family."

"Caitrin, I hate the idea of you being loveless." He stepped forward and embraced me.

My face pressed against his chest, I felt the thrumming of his heart, or maybe it was the pulse of my blood.

"Then show me." Not a whisper of pleading came from me. It was a demand.

"No, I can't," he said and stood back. "I won't do that to you." He held up his hand. "I know you're a grown woman who can make these decisions for herself. And it's a new age. But I won't give in to this simply to satisfy my urges, and yours."

"Don't my urges deserve to be satisfied?" I stepped closer and he backed away. "Thomas." I reached out to his shirt, his muscles outlined by the thin cotton fabric.

"Caitrin," he moaned and closed his eyes.

"I won't regret anything. I promise."

Unsure what to do next, I reached down to his skivvies and grabbed his member.

He jumped back.

"Did I do it wrong?" I stared at the pulsing length.

"Just didn't expect it. There are some steps in between."

"Like what?" I wound my arms around his neck and

kissed him.

He allowed the kiss and even pulled me against his body, warm from the fire and lean. I moved my hands down his back and over his hips to his bulge pressing against my belly.

He chuckled. "You make saying no difficult." He led to me to his bed, tucked into a cozy corner by the fire.

"Everyone says I'm determined." I tilted my chin up and he caressed it.

"I admire that."

The night chill melted in his arms as he kissed me. Our tongues wrestled with a ferocity that I hoped would mean I wouldn't have time to think too much about what I was doing.

It must have worked because before I knew it I was sitting on the edge of his bed, with Thomas kneeling between my legs.

"So soft," he said as his hand slid up the inside of my leg, stopping just short of where the beat of my desire throbbed.

"What do I do?"

"Just touch me." He was the one pleading.

I stroked his back and shoulders. Muscles waved beneath my fingers and his breathing increased. Up close, I could see the scars on his right arm that ran down to his hand. He didn't hide it from me anymore. He pulled off my boots in one motion and placed my ankles on his shoulders, gently laying me back on the bed.

"Thomas?"

"Shh. I think you'll like this." His mischievous grin and wink made me giggle and put me at ease.

I couldn't reach him so I gripped his patchwork quilt as he deliberately placed kisses up my calf and along my thigh. A squeak came out of my mouth as he got closer to my sex. I had heard of this but I figured the girls were making it up.

"Trust me?" He lifted his head and I glanced down.

I nodded and his wicked smile reappeared.

Even though I knew he was going to kiss me there, I wasn't prepared for the sensation.

Lights flashed before my eyes and zips of pleasure streaked though my body. My legs fell open even wider as I dug my nails into the fabric I held on to.

Holding on to the blanket wasn't enough to keep me from coming undone. His tongue and mouth worked some kind of Irish enchantment. When the pressure built, my head thrashed from side to side and I know I screamed his name; I felt the vibrations of it in my throat.

He slid up my body, bunching my nightgown along as he went and pulling it over my head.

"Well, my love?" He brushed my hair from my sweaty face.

"I didn't know it was like that," I panted. "The rest."

"What the lady wants, the lady gets."

Effortlessly, he positioned us the right way on the bed and shed his skivvies. My hand went tentatively to his member.

"Go ahead." He guided me and showed me how to caress him. Although "caress" was too delicate a word; he liked me to squeeze him. I played a finger in his hair and wanted to see all of him.

I tried to surreptitiously lift my head to examine all his parts and I heard him laugh.

"You can look. I'm not ashamed in front of you. I admire your curiosity."

"Do they all look like that?" As I trailed a finger over him, he exhaled and I enjoyed the strain he was under.

"I'm no expert but I like to think I'm an exceptional specimen."

"Hm." I moved both my hands over him.

"Of course, Jewish boys would look different."

"Oh, that's right." I did take a minute to try to cast my mind back to my little cousin's bris, but didn't want to linger too long on that image.

"Caitrin, we can do this a few ways." He took my wrist to still my hand.

"I know how it works. I did go to college." I covered his open lips with a kiss and he pulled me against him. Our bodies fitting together, his length pressing into my belly, sweat making us slick.

He released me slightly. "I only meant we don't have to go all the way."

"Yes, I need to. Besides, don't men get injured if they don't…release?"

His face grew stern. "Don't ever let a boy tell you something like that."

"I know you think you need to protect me." I reached between us and touched him in a way I then knew would render him speechless. "Please." A yearning was building again inside me. Not just a sexual yearning. I needed him to know I was serious about how I was going to live my life and I needed to know how it felt.

Gently rolling me over, he spread my knees apart and settled between them. Supporting himself on his forearms, he cupped my face in his good hand. "I won't get you pregnant."

"I trust you." *I love you.* My eyes flew open at the thought I wouldn't share with him. It was enough to know it myself, that I was giving myself to a man I loved.

His kiss swept me from my body, that and his thumb rotating over the nub of my sex.

I was brought back when the tip of his penis entered me. At first, there was none of the pain that everyone talked about. But then, as he slid farther in, a stretching caused me to yelp as tears pricked my eyes.

"Caitrin. Caitrin. Sorry." Thomas grunted in my ear. "Should I stop?"

I shook my head and gritted my teeth. There was no point in stopping because it was done. Besides, his rubbing had increased and I felt myself about to orgasm again.

I bit down on his shoulder as I tried to clamp my legs together with the wave of coming. He threw his head back and bucked into me. Then he suddenly withdrew and I watched as he spurted out onto my stomach.

He collapsed next to me and grabbed his shirt from the floor. "Sorry." He delicately wiped my belly clean.

"I don't mind."

He embraced me tightly. I didn't care if it was too tight. The flames of the fire were burning down and the air that blew over our bodies caused pricks of goosebumps on my skin.

"You're the most incredible woman I have ever met," he said into my hair.

"You're the most wonderful man I know. I am so glad it was with you. I want to do it again, but not now." A peace descended on my heart. I had crossed a threshold and was no longer scared of what sex was. In fact, I felt stronger for having done it.

"I hope you're not too hurt."

"A little. Will it last long?"

He lifted a shoulder. "I have no idea."

"Really? You've never taken a girl's virginity before?"

"I hate to break it to you, but I'm not as worldly as you might think I am."

"I think you're plenty worldly for me." I lay my head on his chest so I could feel his heartbeat. "Besides, I don't want to think about the world outside this room. At least not for a long time."

Chapter 11

THOMAS

Caitrin's soft body pressed against mine was the most peace I had felt in a long time. And yet it would bring me nothing but heartache, and possibly financial ruin, if she stayed.

"My love, I want nothing more than to hold you until dawn." I kissed the top of her head, her dark curls tickled my nose. I was in her debt now. A position I swore I'd never be in to another person. Being in Caitrin's debt didn't seem too onerous.

"Hmmmm. I don't want to start gossip." She shimmied to the edge of bed and reached for her gown.

"That's going to be hard to avoid." I ran a finger down her smooth back. One last touch to sustain me until we could hide out another few hours.

"Why should it be difficult? We'll just act like we have been." She fumbled with her boots and laced them up.

"I think you're underestimating the attraction we have."

"You sound a little too sure of yourself, Thomas Cullen. If you don't think I can conduct myself in a cool professional way when you're around." She stood, hands on her hips and a playful smile across her lips. It made me want to drag her back into bed. "You've got another think coming."

"We'll see who's making doe eyes from across the office in the morning." I swung my feet over the side of the bed and didn't cover up as I stood to walk her to the door.

Her gaze traveled down, still learning all she could about male anatomy. And I was glad I could be the one to teach her. Her blush stoked my protective instincts, to want to make sure she never learned another man's body. But that would be selfish of me. To keep her from future happiness, simply to satisfy my ego.

She retrieved her quilt from the entryway and I tucked it under her chin.

"Make sure to stick to the edge of the wood. I don't want you spotted coming out of here."

"I will. And don't worry. We're adults and this is no big deal. See you around the office." She tossed her head and stood straight as if we were in the office. Her attempt at bravado failed as she swallowed and blinked back a tear.

Nothing I could do or say would help. With a clear mind, she'd made her choice and I couldn't soften the blow. I would never abandon her or leave her with a baby. But neither could I undo what we just did. And I wouldn't for the world.

"Good night, sweet Caitrin. Have pleasant dreams." I hoped she could have pleasant dreams. I hoped she sensed the growing love I had, and not just the consequences of our act. She wasn't the only one to lose something tonight. No one else would ever take her virginity, and it was likely no one else would ever take my heart.

I took her in my arms and kissed her with the promise

that I adored her, and would care for her for as long as she allowed me.

She didn't say another word and scurried out the door and behind the cottage to take the longer, but more secure route back.

That night, my mind allowed myself pleasant dreams. Dreams of Caitrin in a swimsuit, lounging in one of the adjustable beach chairs, propped up by cloudlike pillows. Her shapely legs tanning in the sun, her skin warmed by the rays.

It took more effort than usual to pull myself out of bed and stand under the frigid spray. Although a cold shower was just the ticket to prepare me to enter the office and see her seated at her desk—efficient, neat, and hiding her wild beauty.

"Mr. Cullen." Ethel Nussbaum came hurrying up to me as I entered the main building.

"Ethel, what's wrong?"

She took a moment to gain her breath. "The gas line to the stove has popped off somewhere. I got Mr. Ronald to help me turn off the gas, but I can't cook anything with no stove. And with no gas, we're not going to be able to use the water heaters that are finally being installed today. I didn't want to complain, you know. But as invigorating as a brisk wash is, it would be nice to soak my feet in some hot water at the end of the day. Not that I want to give up my job. I—"

I held up a hand. "I'll take a look at it right away. But I think I'll hire a building engineer now. There are too many bobs and bits as it is. We'll have to find the funds to hire one now."

I shed my suit jacket and followed Mrs. Nussbaum to the utility shed. Reaching into my past skills, I was able to find the weak connection in the gas line and hook it back up.

The crisis having been averted, I went in search of Ron, who I'd hoped would oversee the plumbers installing the water heaters today. He was either sleeping in, hiding, or off on some errand I hadn't approved.

On the other hand, with Ron out of the way, going over budget to hire an engineer for a few months would be easy. I could explain it much better to Mr. Bergen if it came directly from me, rather than through Ron.

When I did make it to the office, my first order was going to be to Shelley, the newly hired secretary, to place a call for me. Shelley was also mysteriously absent, and I suspected that Ron's small gifts, unctuous compliments, and bragging about his position in his father's business had finally paid off.

I sat at her desk and asked the operator to put me through to Martin's resort.

"Glagorm!"

"Seamus, you'll chase away all of Martin's business with that gravel voice of yours. Can't you add some sparrow song or a little Irish lilt to the way you greet people?"

"It's cold as a witch's teat and I'm the only one minding the place today. Martin and Mary took their niece to the station. She's on her way back to Chicago without a successful Irish husband to bring home to her father."

"Pity. But a bonnie lass like her with her father's wealth

shouldn't have a problem."

"I suspect the father's wealth is more tall tale than dollars in the bank. Otherwise, why'd she have to travel half the earth to come here? But I have no time to gossip like an old lady."

"Neither do I. Can Martin spare you for a few months? I need a strong back and a weak mind to make sure all the new equipment is up and running as it should. I don't have time to fix every loose gas line myself."

"The workers these days don't care about quality job. They come in, rush through installing their piece and are gone before you notice the problems."

"We can sit and lament the mind-set of the modern working man, or you can come earn some money during the season when I know Martin doesn't pay you, but does allow you to stay in that frozen room of yours for free."

A few grumbled off-color phrases made their way to my ear without melting the electric wires. Maybe these wires didn't understand Gaelic.

"So, I'll expect you tomorrow then," I said and hung up before Seamus could follow up with another grumble.

I'd put off entering my office for as long as I could. Gas leak notwithstanding, I could've been there sooner.

"Good morning, Miss Gold." I nodded and hung my coat on the hook.

"Good morning, Mr. Cullen. You are looking rather tired. Did you not sleep well?" Her voice and face were expressionless.

"I slept like a lamb in the spring grass." I tried to match

her tone, but the sunlight coming through the window lit her hair in a halo.

"And I always thought lambs frolicked in the spring."

I choked and coughed.

She took a quick glance up at me and went back to entering the pile of receipts that had accumulated yesterday.

"Were you on the phone just now? Isn't Shelley back from her trip to the city?"

"Why the devil did Shelley go into New York City?"

"Ron sent her. Or maybe he went with her yesterday afternoon. They were meeting with the designer to look at wallpaper samples. Or maybe it was curtains."

"Saints preserve us." I ran my hand through my hair and stared at the ceiling, trying to calm my nerves.

"Your hair is mussed," Caitrin observed.

"My innards are mussed." I shook my head. "Doesn't matter. I have more important things to take care of. I hired Seamus McGillins to be our building engineer for a few months until we take on full staff at the end of spring. With all the workmen in and out, tripping over each other, undoing what the last crew did, I need someone with knowledge and skills to oversee that work, and Ron Bergen is useless at that."

"How much will we be paying Mr. McGillins?" Caitrin opened her ledger and started a new entry.

"I'll work that out with him when he arrives tomorrow. It will probably be about the same as Ethel. Right now, I have to wire Mr. Bergen to explain this decision and hope he doesn't mind the extra expense."

"He'll be here later today." Caitrin continued her calculations, which seemed to take place in her head. I never saw her use the noisy adding machine or scrap paper.

"What do you mean?"

She put down her pencil and looked up. "Ron told me yesterday that his father was coming up to check on things before he and Mrs. Bergen left for Miami for the winter."

I shot up and pounded on my desk. "Did no one think to tell me about this?"

Caitrin remained seated but her eyes went wide. "How was I supposed to know Ron doesn't tell you anything?"

"It's not your fault, Caitrin, uh, Miss Gold. I'm sorry for my outburst." I grabbed my coat back from the hook. It seemed like there was no need to worry about how I would behave around Caitrin today. I wouldn't be in my office enough for it to matter. "I've got to see things are in order for when he gets here." I stopped as I was halfway out of the door. "I appreciate that you finished the ledgers yesterday. Mr. Bergen will be impressed."

Her face lit up with pride. "Thank you, Thomas. Mr. Cullen."

The crises of the day were a blessing. Spending the day making a cottage habitable for Mr. Bergen as well as seeing to the many things I wanted perfect before he arrived would take me away from Caitrin and her rose-scented hair. Although burying my face in her curls would be a much more pleasant way to spend the day. It wasn't likely we'd have another opportunity for a while.

***

CATHY

Thomas ran around like a chicken with its head cut off for most of the day. With the hour of Mr. Bergen's arrival coming closer, he had to make arrangements for a place for him to sleep, a meal fit for him as opposed to the simple fare Mrs. Nussbaum provided, and plan a way to spring the added expense of a new staff person.

As this chaos was going on, Ron and Shelley arrived back from their trip to New York.

"Hello, Cathy. What's buzzin', cousin?" Ron's cheerful demeanor proved that his trip was successful, at least from his vantage point.

"Mr. Cullen is racing around preparing the place for your father. He should be arriving by the four o'clock train."

"That's nearly three hours from now. Plenty of time." His grin was too wide to be sincere.

"Hello, Shelley." I poked my head into her outer office.

I had tried to befriend her in the past few days, but I think she saw me as competition rather than a friend. Not that I would fight her for Ronald Bergen. But it was a shame we couldn't be closer.

"Hiya, Cathy. Wait until you see the fittings we picked out for the cottages. They're aces." She propped herself on the corner of my desk and her smile mirrored Ron's. "You'll never guess what we did yesterday." Without waiting for me to guess she plowed on. "We saw *Kiss Me, Kate*. Oh, the singing was divine. And then we ate at Sardi's and you'll never guess who we saw there."

"Cathy doesn't have time for all this guessing," Ron

interrupted with a weak laugh.

It didn't take much time to guess what Ron and Shelley were up to. More than ever I wished I could share secrets with her.

Her foray with Ron may not have been her first into making love. But that just made me want to talk to her all the more. Was it normal that I felt sore? Would I bleed a little each time we made love? Thomas assured me it wouldn't hurt as much the second time. Loneliness hit hardest when uncertainty edged its way in my mind.

I had considered taking Thomas aside and questioning him. But I lost my courage when he discovered all that needed to be done today. Besides, he would hardly treat me like a typical independent worldly woman if I acted like an innocent ingénue.

I endured a recounting of their New York adventure from Shelley as I did the sums in my head. I found my head was more accurate than my fingers. The adding machine slowed me down with hunting and pecking for the correct keys. And then I had to recheck my work on the paper tape that spewed out its top.

As I was closing up my books, I heard the unmistakable boom of Mr. Bergen's voice.

"That's fine, son. I trust your judgment on this. If we need a tinkerer, we need a tinkerer. And it sounds like he comes cheap enough for the few months he'll be here until we find a more permanent man."

"Thank you, Mr. Bergen. I appreciate your understanding." Thomas entered the office after Mr. Bergen.

"With that gas leak, I felt we had to take some precautions."

"Of course, can't have the place blowing up. Cathy, my *bubbeleh*."

I stood and accepted the hug from Mr. Bergen.

"It's good to see you." As I pulled away, I understood the truth in my words. Mr. Bergen might have been a bit of a blowhard, but he reminded me of my father, and was almost like family. The most familiar face I had seen in a while. "I hope your trip up was easy."

"Trains aren't what they used to be. But let me ask you, how have you been faring? Mr. Cullen not working you too hard?"

"Not at all. The work is easy. I didn't mean to imply it's insignificant. I take my responsibilities seriously."

He placed a hand on my shoulder. "The work is too easy for you. But that's why you're here, to make sure it gets done right. And Thomas filled me in on the ride, he says you've made quick work of it."

"Yes, sir."

"Fine. Why don't we all sit down to dinner in a bit and we can hash out what needs to be done. The season is going to sneak up on us and people will be pouring in expecting great things."

I went back to my cottage to freshen up, using the now-warm water, and joined Mr. Bergen, Ron, and Thomas in the cavernous dining room.

A single round table was set with a white tablecloth that had not been in the list of supplies on hand. Delicate plates and glasses were set for a meal that would apparently be served to us in multiple courses, as opposed to the family style platters Mrs. Nussbaum had been providing.

As talk started, the focus was on the technical side of the resort—the completion of the pool, the last of the painting. Ron and I were largely silent. I had nothing to contribute because it was out of my area of expertise. I suspect it was out of Ron's expertise also.

"Ronald has been a wonderful help in working with the designer. He even went all the way to New York to reiterate the budget constraints." Thomas lifted his glass in a toast to Ron.

"Well done, my boy. Those designers will try to convince you that the resort will completely fail if they don't have the finest Italian marble, or the real gilded-edge picture frames. There's a different between quality and excess. And they get a commission on each piece we buy. So proud that you're on top of it." Mr. Bergen repeated the gesture with his wineglass.

"Yes, well. She took some reining in, but she saw the light." Ron swallowed some of his wine; really, he took a gulp and I might have been the only one to notice it because Thomas and Mr. Bergen had moved on to advertising.

I listened politely until I itched with having to speak up.

"Miss Gold, you seem like you want to contribute something." Thomas nodded at me.

"Thank you. I was only thinking that you can't advertise the Belvedere the same way as Pine Breeze. The synagogue circulars and Yiddish newspapers might be fine for the old resort. But the readerships for those won't be able to afford the Belvedere."

"You're right on the spot there, Cathy." Mr. Bergen stared at me. "I don't suppose you have any ideas."

"I was thinking about my sister's recent wedding. She didn't find anything she used from a newspaper advertisement. It was all about using her best friend's florist, or so-and-so's caterer. We need to get the Belvedere into people's minds. Make it seem like anyone who's anyone will be here this summer."

"Hard to do if no one has been here," Thomas said.

"But I've been here. And Ron's been here." I pointed at Ron, who had been blissfully tucked into his roast and came up for air when his name was mentioned.

"Go on." Thomas put down his fork and gave me his full attention.

"I'll be going back home for a few weeks in December. I'm sure Ron could go home a few times. We can start talking up all the wonderful things we've seen. Daddy certainly can mention it to everyone at the club. We'll generate such word of mouth, people will think they are missing the highlight of the season if they don't book a stay here."

"I like you, Cathy Gold. You've got your mother's brains and your father's cunning. Or maybe it's the other way around. But I am glad you came to work for me. To spreading the word." He lifted his glass and Thomas joined in.

"To Miss Gold."

Ron reluctantly raised his glass about half as high as the

others and took another giant gulp, draining his glass.

"Well, I'd love to stay for Mrs. Nussbaum's desserts. But we have a few odds and ends to take care of so the staff can move into their quarters tomorrow." Thomas wiped his mouth and placed his napkin on the table.

"We're moving?" I dropped my knife and it clattered against the plate.

"Don't tell me you want to stay in the unfurnished cottage with no curtains to block the cold?" Ron slanted his eyes at me. "I would think you'd be happy for a real bed instead of that mattress on the floor."

"Cathy's been sleeping on the floor?" Mr. Bergen glared at Thomas.

"We all have, sir. The staff house wasn't ready yet. But just today, we were able to move the furnishings in." Thomas eyed me with a strong stare.

"That would be much more comfortable." I schooled my expression and tone. But that meant this was the last night with the freedom to come and go as I pleased. The last night to visit Thomas. By tomorrow, there would be Mrs. Nussbaum and Shelley sharing a bathroom and a wing of the staff house. Thomas would have a room among the men's side.

Just when I had found a way to experience love, it was being snatched away.

Chapter 12

THOMAS

Thankful for the excuse of work, I left the dining room. Watching Ron stuff his face while paying no attention to the business Mr. Bergen and I discussed caused Mrs. Nussbaum's roast to sit like a rock in my gut.

Ron would inherit the business, no doubt, and I didn't begrudge him that. It was rightfully his. And even if his older brother had been the one with the natural brains, that didn't mean Ron couldn't grow into the position. His seeming indifference to his privilege was what rankled me. *He* came home in one piece. *He* was still alive. *He* had a father who could leave him an easy life. And all he could do was shove gobs of gravy meat into his maw.

I stopped one of the maids and had her accompany me to the cottage set up for Mr. Bergen. A thorough inspection showed that it lacked a large bath towel and contained an unsightly pile of sawdust left by the workmen. She quickly attended to those items, and I set off for my office for one last check before I gave in to the call my bed had been sending me for the past few hours.

"Psst. Boyo."

I searched the edge of the dark wood for the source of the sound. "Who's there?"

"Me, Garrett."

"Damn it all," I muttered as I stalked to where his form was outlined against a tree. "What the hell are you doing here? Bergen is visiting."

"I know that. Why do you think I'm hiding in the freezing forest?"

I stood close so we could whisper. "So, why are you risking my job?"

"To deliver this." He thrust a sheaf of papers at me.

"I can't read this in the dark."

"It's the deed to the land. Once you sign it and hand over the money, you will be the owner of a piece of America."

"Truly?" I stared at the legal documents, expecting them to evaporate as if it were a dream.

"Yes, sir. It's probably going to wipe out much of your funds, but it will be yours outright. Sorry I wasn't able to convince them to come down in price, but they had to make up for the taxes. And you wouldn't let me ask the bankers to give you a loan."

I waved him off. "I don't want to be indebted to anyone, especially bankers. It'll take a few years, but I'll have the rest to start building on it."

"You're nuts. You should've taken Bergen's offer of an investment."

"No, this is mine." I shook the papers. It hit me. I was a land owner.

Mr. Bergen dining a few yards away didn't deter me. I linked my arm through Garrett's and belted, "Whack fol the dah will ya dance to yer partner. Around the flure yer trotters shake. Wasn't it the truth I told you? Lots of fun at Finnegan's wake."

Garrett twirled me like he was leading the dance and we fell into a fit of laughter.

"Save any of the whiskey for old Seamus McGillins?" The familiar growling voice brought us to a stop.

"Mr. McGillis, we're celebrating young Thomas's status as a landowner." Garrett clapped Seamus on the back and handed him the flask he retrieved from his breast pocket.

Seamus took a long drink, not caring that it wasn't his liquor that was being drunk. "Gone ahead and spent your savings?"

"Yes, and don't judge me for it. I've got land, Seamus. Land. And no one can take that from me, no matter what happens. You're here a night early."

He nodded. "Well, I've unloaded my things in one of them nice cozy rooms you have in the staff house. You invited me not a minute too soon. My old bones are nearly frozen from that drafty barn they keep me in at Galgorm. But this helps." He took another swallow of Garett's flask before handing it back, nearly empty. After two steps away, he turned. "Your father is proud and smiling down on you tonight." He disappeared into the dark, and I didn't swipe the tear away, but let it fall down my face.

"You'd better get going." I pushed Garrett. "And thanks."

"My pleasure, Thomas. Good luck to you." He tipped his hat and skulked off.

Back on the path to my office, I hoped my hand would be still enough to sign my name legibly and then write to Ma and share the good news. Caitrin stepped out of the main building and bundled her coat around her, her breath coming out in little puffs as she took careful steps to her cottage.

By sticking to the edge, I reached the door of her cottage first. "Hey, good looking."

"Oh," she screamed, and I ducked farther into the shadows.

"Shh. Only me."

"Cathy? You okay?" Mr. Bergen's voice sounded from two cottages over where he would be staying.

"Yes, fine. Only an owl scared me. I'll be going to bed now. Good night."

We kept our giggles muffled and she shooed me inside.

I stomped the floor with a jig and lifted her off the ground. "Caitrin, do you know who you are dancing with?"

"A madman who dances when there's no music."

"But there's music in my heart when you're with me. And this." I waved the papers at her.

"Hush, they'll hear you." She pulled away and took the packet, examining it in the moonlight by the window. "Is this the deed to your property?"

"Yes, madam, it is." I bowed and laughed so hard I fell over onto the mattress on the floor.

I didn't care how improper it was to splay on a young woman's mattress in the dark.

"I'm so happy for you. When will you have your inn?" She perched on the edge of her mattress. Close enough for me to caress her arm, but too far for me to kiss her cheek, rosy from the cold.

"That will be a few years from now. Mr. Bergen had offered to invest in the business, but I don't want to be beholden to anyone. I'd rather save the money myself. Let it take a few years, then not owe anyone a dime."

"That's just silly. Even Mr. Bergen takes investors, my father for instance. It makes good business sense to get it off the ground as soon as you can."

"You're probably right. But the only sense I have is that being in debt leads to ruin." I stared at the ceiling. "My father borrowed everything. We didn't own a stick of the furniture we used. And it was all seized away. I won't let that happen to me or my family." I turned to look at her. "When I have a family."

She looked away. "Thomas, what kind of mother or wife would I be if I was at an office for hours each day?"

I slid over to her and nuzzled her delicate neck. "I think you'd make a wonderful mother and wife."

"Don't," she pleaded.

"You want me to stop?" I pulled away.

"No. But don't ask for more than we can have." Her eyes turned down. "I want you. I want to have as much time together as we can."

I followed the line of her temple, down her cheek and neck, over her collarbone, and dipped into the front of her blouse.

"Are you sure?" Gazing into her whiskey-brown eyes, I realized nothing could disappoint me in that moment. I would take whatever Caitrin would give, and content myself with that.

"Yes. I'm sure. But I'm a little…" Her face flamed red.

"Oh, yes." She was still in some pain from last night. "Well, how about we try something different."

She nodded and immediately peeled off my jacket. Her enthusiasm for anything she liked outshone any proper manners she may have been taught. Whether it was work or making love, she did it with all her soul.

Gently taking each button through its hole, I exposed her skin and ran my hand over her breasts, still encased in one of those god-awful brassieres.

"If I could, I would invent an undergarment for women that wasn't a fortress."

"I think anything you invented would magically open with that mischievous look of yours." She reached behind her and unclasped her bra. Her full breasts sprung out, and with a sigh, she allowed me to lick her nipples into hard peaks. Rolling one around my mouth and lightly pinching the other brought forth rumbles from her throat.

I reluctantly left off stroking her breast to undo her skirt. With one hand it was difficult and I couldn't work the baffling fastening that ladies' clothes seemed to have.

"Why don't you use your other hand to help?"

I stopped and looked up at her. Her eyes demanded that I use my right hand and what fingers were left there.

"Don't keep that hand hidden all the time. If I'm giving my body to you, then you have to give me your entire body as well."

Clearly, she wasn't going to allow me to go any further unless I took my bad hand from under my side where I kept it so it wouldn't disgust her.

"Well?"

I took a deep breath and I still had my entire right thumb and little finger. With them and the bottom parts of my other fingers, I had gotten fairly adept at small things. Caitrin relaxed back down and allowed me to undress her.

Her stunning body reflected the slice of moonlight through the window, and her skin prickled in the cold. She unbuttoned my shirt and pulled off my undershirt, humming in appreciation as she did so. My skin didn't feel the cold at all. Not with her fiery gaze on me.

"Let me warm you up." I stroked her skin and kissed between her breasts.

Her chest rose and fell each time my lips skimmed her body. Need coiled in my groin, but this was about pleasing Caitrin. Showing her how good love could be, and hopefully, leaving her wanting a bit more in the future.

"Yes," she whispered as my mouth neared her sex.

I could already catch her musky scent. I separated her folds and ran my tongue up her slit.

"Oh." She wriggled against her mattress and dug her hands into my hair. "Please again."

Lick after lick she bucked more. I slipped one finger inside her tight channel, which brought out a wanton moan. With tender sucks at her bud it took her no time at all before she came. Wild thrashing of her head and a near piercing of my skin as she gripped my shoulder brought its own kind of satisfaction to me. A final buck of her hips and she pulled away.

She curled to her side and pulled me up to hold her. "I can't believe that."

"Mmm." I rested my chin on her head, her crazy curls dancing across the quilt.

"Doesn't seem fair to you."

"When you're feeling up to it," I said and kissed her ear.

"But can't I? I mean I've heard…"

"Caitrin. Where did you hear of that?"

"I did go to college." She propped herself on her elbow and placed a hand on her hip.

"I'm sure that Vassar College doesn't offer a course of study in *that*."

"Then you'll have to show me." She undid my fly before I could even respond.

"I-I-Caitrin."

"Shouldn't you lie back?" She pushed at my chest and knelt between my knees. "Show me."

Unsure exactly how to demonstrate since it was physically impossible, I held my erection up and she cautiously took it in her hand.

"You won't hurt me," I assured her.

She began at the base and licked up in one long stroke, her wet mouth leaving a path of heat. Over and over her small tongue tortured me. The urgency built, but no release would come with her timid ministration.

"Here." I wrapped my hand around hers and showed her to increase the pressure.

"So tight?"

I nodded and groaned as she pumped.

"Should I do this?" She covered the top with her sweet lips.

I think I called out a "yes" but it might have been simply a noise of approval. Her petite hand continued to clench me as her mouth laved liquid heat.

My coil came undone and with a grunt, I pulled away, coming over her fingers. The release settled in my gut and left me.

"Am I not supposed to taste it?"

My head swam with answers, none of them right for a young woman. She dipped her head and flicked her tongue once.

"Hmm. Really salty." She squirmed up and lay alongside me. "I guess I did it right."

"Mmmm. You might need more practice." I opened one eye and grinned.

"Oh, you're horrible." She swatted my arm.

"I am horrible." I pulled her against me. "But I'd like for you to let me be less so. Let me be honorable. Make an honest woman—"

"Shh." She placed her finger on my lips. "No. Let's just be us. Working to get this beautiful place open. I don't want to think about what comes next."

I didn't want to think about that either. It was difficult to think about anything as the cold air blew across my perspiration. My land, my girl, my job. None of them fit with each other. But for now, it was enough.

***

CATHY

"Golly, those men are making quick work of it, aren't they?" Shelley gazed out the window off the unfinished lobby at the whirlwind of workers. She had decided I wasn't a rival for Ron, and so we had fallen into a friendly companionship. Although still not close, we could play three-handed bridge with Mrs. Nussbaum in the evening and listen to the radio

"I hear it might snow next week. That's enough to spur them on to finish the structures, before they can move inside."

"I know I'm looking forward to warming up over this break. These places aren't made for this time of year. Aren't you homesick?" She fingered a stand a pearls I hadn't seen before. Those along with a silk scarf had to come from Ron, who couldn't be earning enough for all of that. I hoped they would be happy together if Ron's gifts and trips into New York dried up.

"I miss my family." As I said it, I wondered if it were true. For three weeks, I'd be at home on Long Island spending time with Mom and Daddy. Beth would be home from boarding school and we would go to party after party. I'd be introduced to boy after boy. But if I could drum up business for the Belvedere, it would be worth it.

"Miss Gold." Thomas struck his professional stance. I could distinguish it from his more casual tone and posture of those stolen moments alone in his office. "Would you accompany me on an errand? I have to go choose towels from the wholesaler, and I'm sure to pick out the most sandpaper-like ones if I don't have a woman's touch."

"I'm sure that's not true. Your attention to every detail is impeccable. But if I can help," I said and followed him to the office to get our coats. In those brief times together, he would share stories of his childhood and quote some poems by heart that always seemed to be the perfect reflection of my mood. We strategized about the resort, each exciting the other with a new idea.

"Thanks for inviting me," I said as we entered the office. "I could use some air. It's probably the last day it will be fit to be outside. Let me put away…" I searched on my desk for the bills and receipts I had wanted to get to next.

"Have you misplaced something?" Thomas came up behind me and as always, our tiny office seemed too small to maintain a respectable distance. Any space I shared with Thomas would seem too small to be respectable.

"I can't find the receipts and bills I had piled up here." I stepped into the outer office where Shelley had returned. "Shelley, you haven't seen yesterday's receipts. Have you?"

"I think Ron—Mr. Bergen had them."

"Thanks." I walked through her space to Ron's office. "Ron? Do you have the bills I was working on?"

He slammed shut his desk drawer. "Yes, right here. I was simply putting a report together for my father."

"And you still haven't handed me the decorator's receipts. All I have are these notes from meetings you've had with her."

"Oh, you know those artsy types." Ron waved. "She doesn't give receipts. It's all verbal understanding with her."

I shook my head. "Did you talk to Thomas about this? Or your father?"

"My father knows all about this. He's used this decorator for years."

I did remember Mr. Bergen talking about this decorator. I seemed to recall Mom had hired her for our addition to the house.

I took the sheaf of papers from his hand, but something didn't add up. Ron wouldn't do one bit of work more than he had to. And making a report for his father didn't make sense.

I replaced the bills in my desk and followed Thomas to the van.

The wind nearly blew me off my feet, but Thomas's hand held my arm as we walked into the gusts and the warmth of the van.

"Whew, that's some wind," he exclaimed as he turned the car to life.

"I can only imagine what January will be like."

"You won't like it one bit."

"Especially because we can't find any time for you to warm me." I placed my hand over his as he held the steering wheel.

"Caitrin, love." His voice was soft with the longing and sadness we both felt.

"Let's talk about something else," I said, aching at the tone of his voice. "Is Ron spying on us? Do you think Mr. Bergen asked him to check on what we're doing?"

Thomas shrugged. "I have no idea. Mr. Bergen has

always trusted me. At least he said he has, and has never given me any reason to think otherwise. But this is a big undertaking and the stakes are high. If Ron is reporting back to Bergen, it gives Ron something to do besides get in the way, and I've nothing to hide."

"I have nothing to hide either, but still I worry what Ron was doing with my papers."

"He got me suspicious earlier as well. But no worrying today." Thomas placed his hand on my knee and gave it a squeeze. "I have something special to show you."

"I knew this wasn't simply about towels." I laughed and held his hand in place. I could barely feel his warmth through the many layers I wore. But touching freely buoyed my emotions.

"We are going to purchase towels, but first, enjoy the scenery."

"The trees are bare. The sky is a dull gray. The birds are gone. Not even a snowfall yet," I teased.

"Pardon me," he said. "It must be me with the beautiful view, as I can gaze at you all I want with no one around."

A tear sweetly stung my eye. "You're lucky you are driving," I choked. "Or I'd fling my arms around your neck and smother you with kisses."

"I'll be stopping the car in a few moments." He winked.

We drove along the main road until we came to a small clearing where he pulled off and stopped the van.

"We're nowhere," I said.

"Come." He got out and came around to open my door and help me down.

With his arm through mine, he guided me along what was barely a path. More of a crossing for deer. I was hoping we were finding a secluded spot to share affections, but worried that the cold would prevent us from sharing enough.

Then the woods opened up and we were on Liberty Lake, only on the far side from Pine Breeze.

"Thomas," I gasped. "Is this your land?"

"Yes, my love. You're standing on the private property of Thomas William Cullen. And you are trespassing."

My mouth opened to exclaim my excitement but I found Thomas's lips on mine.

The passionate kiss melted the nipping air. I fell into his arms and let him guide me to the ground.

"Thomas. Not here in the winter?"

"You wanted to in the summer." He continued to kiss along my neck, nudging aside my scarf.

"We'll freeze." My protest was halfhearted at best.

"You have so little faith in my lovemaking that I won't keep you warm." He took my hand and pulled me to my feet, and then we walked deep into the woods.

"What's that?" I asked as a dilapidated shack came into view.

"That is why the Catskills are the Catskills. It's an old stillhouse. During Prohibition, our Irish and Jewish gangster ancestors would hide their hooch in the wilderness of the mountains. Either smuggled in from Canada or distilled right here."

The door still hung on the hinges, but the roof tilted. When we stepped in, I saw someone had cleared the floor and laid a new mattress on top of a tarp.

"It's not our elegant digs, but I thought it would do."

"Oh, Thomas." And those were the last words I was able to utter for a good thirty minutes.

Lying alongside him, the heat of our bodies dissipating into the cold air, I breathed in the scent of pine needles and his skin.

"We'd best bundle up." Thomas righted my clothes and buttoned my coat before fixing his pants.

"I wish we had more time together." I tipped my head up and looked out through the hole in the roof to the bare branches.

"It's the preciousness of our times together that make them so important. Unless you've changed your mind and will allow me to make you mine." He kissed my nose before wrapping my scarf back around my chin.

"Please, don't ask me that. Let me make these decisions."

He nodded. "Now that we have christened my land, we'd better buy some towels."

I giggled. "Is this how the Irish christen their land?"

"I have no idea. The Irish don't own much of their own land to begin with. Certainly no one in my family ever has."

"Your mother must be very proud of you."

He nodded and helped me to stand. "I wrote her when I signed the deed. I expect she'll have the neighbors over for a celebratory nip."

"And your father would be very proud."

"Well, he's looking down at me now and saying

'Tommy, what's in your fool head? You've got that piece of land and it's not fit for planting rye.' But he's saying it with love."

"I think I would have liked your father." I allowed Thomas to guide me into the passenger seat.

He paused and considered. "He wasn't always an easy man to like. But he was a hard worker. If a short-sighted one. He never thought more than a week away. And sometimes not even that far. Never saw possibilities, good or bad. And that's why he died in debt, leaving me to pick up the pieces."

He shut the door and walked to the driver's side. Admiring Thomas for overcoming his humble beginnings was easy. Knowing how to talk to him about them was hard.

"I've had a pretty easy life. It makes me feel guilty for complaining."

"There's nothing easy about living a life you don't want. Being trapped in that brilliant mind of yours isn't easy. We all have our crosses to bear. Oh, sorry. I didn't mean to bring up crosses."

We were off again, headed toward the areas where factories produced anything the city people needed.

"Don't be sorry. It's just an expression. That's one thing I don't feel guilty for, no matter how many people would like to blame the Jews for that biblical act thousands of years ago."

"Not thousands yet, just under two thousand years, love. We'll be old and gray and dandling grandchildren when that two-thousand mark of our savior's, my savior's, birth comes around."

"Grandchildren?" The sting of this tear was bitter instead of sweet.

"I didn't mean…"

"It's all right. Once you have your business up and running, you'll be a catch for any beautiful girl you want. And this bookkeeping job will give me enough money to start my life in New York. I'll get the kind of job I want and…and I'll always treasure what we shared."

His jaw was clamped shut, eyes unmoving from the point in the distance. He took a turn a little too sharply, but I didn't flinch.

I was angry too. The uselessness of giving in to that anger outmatched any good that could come from railing against my impossible situation.

We passed a canning plant and some other flat-roofed brick building, where men with blackened faces and rough hands stood outside for a few gulps of clean air before returning to whatever spot on an assembly line they called their occupation.

"See those factories? Those machines? They take the life out of people. Not just your physical life, but your soul. I'm never going back, just as you're not going to go back to your father's home." He took a deep breath. "The weavers are over here." Thomas parked the car next to the delivery trucks with the towel company logo on the side.

We rushed into the offices and pulled the door closed behind us as the wind had picked up.

"Hello, Mr. Cullen. It's good to see you again." A

peppy blonde woman lit up as we walked in.

"Hello, Miss Phillips. This is my accountant and bookkeeper, Miss Gold. She's here to ensure the products I choose meet with feminine standards."

"You know I'm happy to give you my assistance in that area whenever you need it."

I ground my teeth, because I was fairly certain Miss Phillips had shared her feminine standards with Thomas before. But maybe it was simply territorial on my part.

We were brought into a showroom where a clerk displayed a range of towels in sizes and weaves. At first, I listened intently to his explanations of thread quality and weave density. But then I decided feeling the towels was probably the easiest thing.

"Oooh." I ran my hand over a towel clearly made from a cloud.

"Well, yes, that's our top of the line. And nothing short of that would do for Mr. Bergen's new resort." The clerk's eyes had dollar signs in them.

"Mr. Bergen is a savvy businessman. He looks for value as well as quality." Thomas was able to put a friendly tone into any rejection.

"What are those?" I pointed to a pile of multicolored towels at the end of the counter.

"Those are some of our custom dyed and monogrammed pieces." The clerk brought over the towels.

"Thomas, what if each cottage had its own color scheme?" I asked. "There's always a fight over towels at Pine Breeze. You put your towel down and someone is bound to snatch it up when you go into the water."

"You've got an eye for these things." Thomas went into negotiations with the clerk about how many patterns and colors they could provide, and surely, there must be a discount for a customer as loyal as Mr. Bergen.

Once the order was placed and hands shaken, we walked out past Miss Phillips.

"Mr. Cullen, will you be attending the Christmas Ball this year? We had such a fine time last year, and with rations lifted I'm sure the refreshments will be even better."

"I'm not sure, Miss Phillips. The Belvedere is keeping me busy, and I've obligations."

"Of course. I'll save a dance for you if you come." She beamed a brilliant smile through perfectly lipstick adorned lips.

I held my tongue until we were in the van.

"I know I have no standing to comment about your past, or your future. But I don't think Miss Phillips suits you."

"No?" Thomas asked with a grin.

"I think she's not nearly intelligent enough for you."

"You could gauge her intellect from that brief time?"

"I could tell she was interested in landing a husband so she doesn't have to work at the towel factory. Her makeup case took up more room on her desk than her typewriter. And I spotted three fashion magazines poking out from under the pad of dictation she should have been working on."

"Not everyone is as diligent or as smart as you." His

mouth turned up in a sad grin. "I'm not interested in Miss Phillips, the wayward towel company secretary. But you won't have me. What am I to do?"

"It's not that I *won't* have you, it's that I *can't* have you."

"I think you can have anything you want, my love."

We traveled in silence for the rest of the way back to the Belvedere. The temperature had dropped both outside and inside the van.

My mother's path in life proved that I couldn't have anything I wanted. Even above-average intelligence couldn't change the realities of the world.

Chapter 13

THOMAS

If baby Jesus was born in a manger, I shouldn't grouse about the drafty rooms of the staff house. Although we had a skeleton staff, the three weeks I gave everyone off meant the staff house felt even colder.

Only Seamus and I rattled around, and we stayed in as few rooms as possible so as to easily keep the fires going.

"Stop mooning about. She'll be back in another week." Seamus poured a liberal dose of his good whiskey and offered it to me.

"I could pretend I don't know who you are talking about." I swallowed the liquor that burnt going down, but warmed my gut.

"Gah. The only one you are fooling is that dimwit Ronald. But you'd need to take out an advertisement in the newspaper for him to figure it out. If he can read." He pushed his feet out to the crackling fire.

"I'll make sure we're more discreet." I finished the whiskey and didn't ask for more. Not because I was being polite. But because it didn't seem right to get drunk on Christmas Eve.

"Oh, you're discreet. But a blind man wouldn't miss the way you two look at each other over the dinner table. Like the rest of us are eating plain bread and you both are supping on manna."

"I love her, Seamus. I can't help it. I know we have no future together. She's gone right at the start of the season and I'll make the most of every moment we have."

Seamus grunted and pushed himself out of the chair. "You about ready?"

"Ready?"

"It's Christmas Eve and St. Michael's is having midnight mass. Get your boots and muff." He strode to the door. "You've got to drive an old man to church on what might be his last Christmas Eve on this earth. You wouldn't want me going to meet St. Peter and have to explain why I didn't celebrate the birth of our lord. He who brought peace to the world and love to all men. So get up off your lazy rusty dusty and get the car warmed up before I slap ya."

"You've been promising to die since I've known you." I stood and followed him to the door.

"Hmph. 'A promise is a debt.' And I don't owe you a thing."

"No. I am in your debt. What would I have done without you after Da passed away?"

He shrugged. "I was simply doing what any decent sort does when they can do it. Like you taking me to church. If we ever get there. Fancy women take less time to get ready."

"When you do get to the pearly gates, you'll bully St Peter into letting you in. I wouldn't worry about making it to church."

The roads were lightly frosted and I took care in

driving. We didn't talk much except to run down the list of chores left to be done before the decorator arrived and we took delivery of all we'd ordered.

Caitrin had even more brilliant ideas as we planned and plotted. The Belvedere would be a jewel in Mr. Bergen's crown, and as a result, a boon to me. My place would never be grand, but my work would boost my reputation, and I was hoping for a bonus at the end of the year, a few extra dollars toward my own construction. I was so close I could taste it.

Whenever Caitrin and I visited my land, we did more than just make love. I'd describe my plans. She'd improve on them. More often than I wanted to admit, I envisioned her standing beside me as we opened the inn. But she just as frequently talked of her dreams—an apartment in Manhattan, a job where she earned enough to travel and go to the opera. At her young age, she had already given up a dream of a family. Not that I could blame her. When I thought of Maggie back home, I wished for her to be able to support herself as well. But I would make a fine uncle.

Organ music wafted out of the small Catholic church, the only one around. Flickering lights glowed through the windows. And we stepped over a few heaps of snow to get to the entrance.

The Irish and Italians had to get along at church. There wasn't enough of either one of us to make a go of separate churches. And with the mass in Latin, no one knew what was being said anyway.

Seamus found some friends in a pew and joined them. I

motioned to the chapel with the Blessed Virgin and he nodded. I took a few coins from my pocket and dropped them in the box. I lit a candle for my father and looked into the statue's face.

I hope you're watching over him. Da was never very good at watching over himself. Although, I suppose now that he has eternity ahead of him, he doesn't need to think about the future. Make sure he knows I'm setting up my future. And Maggie's. We're both well and…and. Just tell him we know he did the best he could in making sure we were born in this land where we had a chance.

I joined Seamus in the pews and let the mass flow in one ear and out the other. God knew my heart, and He didn't care much if I paid attention.

I wondered what Caitrin was doing with her family now. Even if we were able to overcome the obstacles of her dreams and mine, even if we brought down some miracle and her father didn't object to her marrying a poor man who never finished school, there was no way we could find a place in the world that would take us. What would she do on Christmas Eve while Seamus and I went to mass? And what would I do when…when. Well, the Jewish people did other things that I'm sure I could never take part in. If we had children, would the boys come to church with me and the girls be raised as Jews?

A short burst of laughter came out, which caused a few heads to turn and Seamus to elbow me in the ribs.

The absurd thoughts made it clear. We had no future past this coming summer. I wouldn't stand in Caitrin's way, and my future didn't include her. In heaven, it doesn't matter if you're rich or poor, educated or unschooled. Maybe it also doesn't matter which god you pray to. Maybe Caitrin and I shared a future somewhere not on this earth.

***

CATHY

The blisters on my feet had better pay off in guests in the cottages.

I discreetly rubbed my foot under the table. Decked out in gold for New Year's Eve, the Rosemere Country Club hummed with music, laughter, and a band that played slow versions of familiar songs.

Thankfully, this was my last party before I could return to Pine Breeze. I had impressed my family by accepting every invitation to every social event. Chanukah dance at the temple, snowball dance at the alumni club. That's not even counting the endless smaller gatherings I attended. Every high school and college friend within driving distance had seen my smiling face and heard my wondrous tales of building a Catskills resort.

Their eyes were filled with images of opulence. They could almost feel the lush towels and crisp linens. The light danced off the china, the description of the sample menus woke taste buds to new experiences. And as soon as one person showed interest, I used that name with the next person. And so on, until it seemed as if the entire world was eager to visit.

They all begged their fathers and husbands to book a stay at the Belvedere.

The thought that kept me going through all of this was

the stories I could share with Thomas when I got back. How we'd laugh. He would pull me close, tucked under his arm as we gazed out at Liberty Lake from the edge of his property. He'd congratulate me and tell me I had a future in advertisement.

"Cathy, it's so wonderful that you've thrown yourself into all these social events." Mom sat next to me at our regular table we shared with the Bergens, who had come up for a few parties, but were returning to Miami as soon as they could.

"I have to get all my socializing in before going back up to the Belvedere. It's deserted up there." My approach with my parents was I would finish the job because I promised Mr. Bergen, but they were right, I needed to be among more people. And then when they weren't looking, whamo, I'd have my own apartment and a job in New York City.

They didn't need to know how much I missed the quiet. The peaceful winter sounds. The cozy fires. Even Shelley's inept card playing was a welcome treat at the end of a long day. I would have to trade the quiet life for city life in order to have a career. But it was a sacrifice I was willing to make.

"And here are the rest of my beauties." Daddy brought over an extremely reluctant Beth on one arm and a smiling if distracted Marilyn on the other. "I've got the photographer here. I want a photo with all of us."

"Smile for just a few seconds, would you please, Beth." Mom fussed with Beth's hair.

"The money spent on this event could plant orchards

of date trees in Israel."

"I'll send some dates to the Holy Land. Sit next to your mother," Daddy ordered.

We posed for a few pictures before Marilyn scampered off to sit with all her married friends.

"Even Cathy has gotten into the holiday mood." Daddy drank some wine. "I'm impressed. I bet you've been starved for company."

"It can get lonely. But the resort is coming along so well."

"Please, no more about the paradise of bourgeois excess." Beth rested her face in her hands until a stern look from Mom brought her to correct posture again.

"I'm proud of you, Cathy. I honestly didn't realize that you would take to the work so well. And it's put me at ease to know my investment is going to pay off."

"Everyone has been talking about it," Mom agreed.

I was spared from any more fibs when a poor unsuspecting boy from the temple was nervously pushed forward by his mother to ask Beth to dance. She might have strong opinions, but she wasn't cruel and wouldn't reject a boy who so obviously had rehearsed his lines. Besides, even a Socialist needs to find love.

I shared a smile with Mom as we watched their retreating backs.

"Look, there's Will Hartman." Daddy waved Will over and Mom caught my defeated expression.

"Happy New Year, Mr. and Mrs. Gold. And Happy New Year, Cathy. You look lovely."

"Happy New Year, Will."

It seemed no one would end the awkward moment. "Ask me to dance, Will. I've not been up yet."

"Of course." He took my hand and guided me to the floor.

"Sorry about my father," I said as we swayed about.

"It's okay. My parents are the same way. I hear you're personally hammering in each nail of that new resort."

"Ha ha. No, just keeping the accounts. But I am learning a lot about business." I had known Will my entire life, and he was being a good sport about my not accepting his courtship. "Can you keep a secret?"

"Yes, but that's because no one ever asks me anything." He smiled.

"I'm going to keep working. Even after the Belvedere is up and running. My parents don't know this yet, but I'm saving my salary and I'll be able to afford an apartment in New York until I find work."

"I'm not surprised. You always had irregular plans." He looked past my shoulder. "I don't suppose you are looking for a marriage proposal or anything like that."

"Oh, Will. I'm not. But you're a wonderful guy and if I were looking for a proposal, it would be from you." I kept any tears at bay as he turned to look at me. I hated hurting him, and the white lie might soften the blow.

He nodded and kept his jaw clamped shut, then smiled his sad smile. "I'm happy for you. You don't need to lie to me. But if it's worth anything, I'd only ever want to marry a friend."

"You will. I know you will. Thanks for understanding. Besides, could you picture me as the happy homemaker?"

We laughed, but I had to force mine. There was one person I could be happy with, at least in my dreams.

"I'm telling you this, not just because we're old friends."

He winced slightly at the "old friends" but kept a brave face.

"You're working in insurance aren't you?"

"Yes, got a lot of good accounts. I'm very well set." He expressed his pride as if to let me know what I was missing out on.

"I want to work as an actuary. I wonder if you can put in a good word for me with Mr. Blum. He's an investor of Mr. Bergen's. Once he sees how great the Belvedere is, I know he'll want to hire me. You don't owe me anything. And maybe I'm overstepping myself…"

Will's gaze stayed out past my shoulder, then softened. "No, you're not overstepping. I'm very new myself, but if I see the opportunity to talk to Blum, I'll put in a good word for you."

"Oh, Will, you've made my day. My year."

"The year is just a few hours old," he said. "But I do wish you well, Cathy. And I'll do what I can."

I nearly kissed him from gratitude, but came to my senses.

The song ended and he brought me back to my parents.

"Well, well. I saw you light up in Will Hartman's arms." Daddy grinned. "Maybe it's not too late."

Mom's confusion played across her features, but I didn't answer her questioning look.

"I'm just happy to see 1949 start. It's got to be better than the past few years."

"I'll toast to that." Daddy raised his glass.

There was no guarantee Will would help me find a position. But this was the start. I was taking control of my own destiny. My future was in my hands. A little bit of money and I could own my life. I could have anything I wanted. Except the one thing that had been making me happy for the past six months.

Chapter 14

THOMAS

The green buds and chirping sparrows echoed the joy in my heart. Final preparations were on schedule for the Belvedere, despite Ron's last-minute changes with the designer. Mr. Bergen had been up from New York a few times and was more than pleased, both with the progress of the resort and with how Ron seemed to have fallen into taking on new responsibilities. I never did ask him about Ron's secretive reports he had told Caitrin about. But Mr. Bergen was a straight shooter, he'd ask me anything he wanted to know.

It wasn't the impending opening of the Belvedere, or the budding spring that had my heart skipping beats. It was Caitrin Gold. That girl was something else. Not only had she grown into a passionate lover, she lived each day with gusto. She knew that in a matter of weeks, she'd be gone. We'd already hired someone for the bookkeeper position. A sturdy local man, who'd left part of his leg on an island in the Pacific and returned to find his sweetheart waiting for him. He had finally finished healing and was eager for work.

He wasn't nearly as pretty at Caitrin, or as quick and bright. But he'd do now that she had put everything in place.

"Mail is here." Shelley handed me a stack.

"Thanks, Shelley." I took the letters and spotted one

from Mrs. Clatchy. Today was the day I would start with Ma's letter. Too many things were running smoothly for me to deny myself a moment of good news from home.

I entered my office to the sound of Caitrin singing a tune from the movie we had seen last week. She had a duster and was cleaning the shelves and jiggling as she sang.

"I'm gonna wash that man right out my hair, and send him on his waaaay."

I gritted my teeth at the last note, because Caitrin might have the face of an angel, but I predicted they would never let her sing in the heavenly choir.

"You're not sending someone packing, are you?"

"Oh. I thought you were training the new engineer."

"All done. Harold's a natural, genius really. The army trained him well. If he were white, he'd be using one of those GI Bills to go to college. Don't tell Seamus I said I liked the new guy so much." I sat at my desk and flipped through the rest of the mail.

"Is he happy to be back in his regular room?" She stood on her tiptoes to reach the high shelf and I shamelessly eyed her bottom as she flexed.

"Seamus is never happy. But I suppose he's more comfortable back with Martin."

She sneezed at the dust and turned around. "Some people can never live outside their own world." Her eyes were red either from dust or from what her words really meant.

"He's old and set in his ways. I've learned to live very happily here. I even learned to like gefilte fish."

"No one likes that." She perched on the edge of my desk.

"Maybe we'll steal away for a picnic lunch?" I winked.

"Mr. Cullen, I always enjoy your picnics." She slid off my desk and sashayed to hers, taking her seat with exaggerated motions and allowing her adorable leg to poke out. She fluttered her eyelashes for good measure.

"We'll have a fine picnic today." I couldn't suppress my grin. I sliced open the envelope from Ireland expecting to read Ma's words through Mrs. Clatchy's neat penmanship.

But this letter began differently. Mrs. Clatchy had written to me directly. The words swam before my eyes, and it wasn't what I had always feared. Apparently, Ma and Maggie were well. Healthy and happy. If you can call scrubbing floors for others happy.

…and I couldn't go on letting you believe that your Mother, God bless her, was using your hard-earned American money for Maggie's education. She hasn't been to school in years. The money was never really enough, but your poor mother never wanted to hurt your feelings. She knows how you took responsibility for the family at a young age. She didn't want you to worry. She's been lying to you, believing it's for your own good. But I could imagine you'd want to know the truth, seeing as your father was a hard man and would have never lied. It does a disservice to his memory…

There was more, but I couldn't take it in. The omelet Mrs. Nusbaum had made churned in my gut. A pounding that had begun in my ears thundered through my body. I crumpled the letter and pounded my fist into the desk. The pain wasn't enough, so I did it again.

"Thomas. What's wrong?" Caitrin stood and approached.

I pushed back my chair and shoved her out of the way. I had to get out, get air, be alone. Tears were coming. Angry tears and some Gaelic curses. I flat out ran to the woods, pushed my way through the early growth, deep into where the creatures scurried away from me.

After running, my clothes in tatters from the brush, I stopped. Panting, sweating. The scream that issued from my mouth tore the air. Branches shook with the flight of birds. It wasn't enough so again and again I screamed. I screamed for the lies and deceit. I screamed for my own gullible heart. And I screamed for Maggie's lost years. At fifteen, she would be married off to some farmer with more rocks than soil to his name. Dependent on how long his back was strong and how many healthy sons she could raise.

Exhausted, I sank to the ground, the dampness seeping through my pants. I leaned against a rough tree. This suit would have to be thrown away, past mending. All my money had been enough just to keep them going. I swiped at my face, because I wouldn't allow any more tears. Tears were too salty to grow ideas.

They would have to come back. Maggie was an American, born here in New York State. She had every right to be here, and I could get Ma a job at Martin's resort, or some other Irish place. Maggie could attend the local school. It would nearly empty my account to get them tickets. Maybe Martin could let Maggie live there and work after school for her keep. Summer was approaching, there would be no school for a while. If it meant putting off my dreams for a few more months, so be it. My land was mine. I wouldn't sell it. The inn would wait.

I stayed there for a while longer, allowing the wildlife to come back. In the stillness, a doe and her twin fawns nervously nibbled on young shoots. Peace. The countries were at peace with each other. The world was at peace with the spring. I wasn't ready to forgive Ma. But Maggie wouldn't suffer because of my anger or Ma's misguided decisions.

When my heart beat comfortably in my chest, I realized I'd have to explain everything to Caitrin. What a fool she would think I was. And her opinion of my family would certainly slip. Not that she would be likely to meet Maggie and Ma. She'd likely be gone by the time they arrived.

I stood and brushed off what I could of the leaves and dirt. It took me a good twenty minutes to return. I wasn't sure if that was because I had lost my way or if I had run so far that walking back it took twice as long.

Caitrin, Ron, and most of the staff were assembled outside. Caitrin issued orders and was pointing when she spotted me.

I held up my hand to stop her from running into my arms. Not in front of everyone else.

"I'm sorry, everyone, for causing you concern. No need to form a search party. I had some unsettling news from my family in Ireland. Give me a few minutes to change my clothes and I'll be back in the office soon. I think Mr. Bergen can handle any questions in the next little while. Is that okay?" I looked to Ron, hoping for once to see a light of intelligence.

"Of course. I'll work with the kitchen staff on menus."

I nodded, and waited for the staff to return. Caitrin stayed put. Her hands on her hips, her eyes a mix of concern and doubt.

"Meet me in the office after I've changed." My voice was hoarse from the screaming, but also from keeping my emotions in check now that I had her lovely face to comfort me.

"If you're not there in ten minutes, I'm calling the sheriff with his tracking dogs." She attempted a satisfied smile, but her quivering lips told me she was as concerned as I was.

I might have been more than ten minutes but not much. My underclothes were salvageable, but the rest would be for rags. Washing my face and adding some Brylcreem to my hair helped me look better, even though the scratches on my face from the brambles were still bright red.

Caitrin nervously tapped a pencil on desk and she jumped when I came in. She didn't bother about the impropriety of closing the door behind me.

"Thomas." She flew into my arms and her warm breath against my chest threatened to start the tears again.

"Caitrin, I'm sorry I was like that. I shouldn't have pushed you. I…"

"Just tell me what happened," she said into my now best, formerly second best, suit coat.

I cleared my throat and pulled back. "Sit down." I

motioned to her chair and sat in the visitor chair, unable to sit at my desk with the still-crumpled note atop.

"My mother has been lying to me. She's been taking my money meant for Maggie's education and they've been using it to simply live."

"How can that be? You said you got reports."

I reached over and smoothed the letter. "For the first few years, Maggie did go to school. But for the past couple, she's had to work cleaning houses, just like Ma. They nearly starved and Ma didn't want me to be disappointed or give up saving for my inn."

"You must be angry and worried all at the same time."

I laughed. "You understand me too well, sweetheart." I touched her arm. I wanted to touch more, not for lust, for comfort. I wanted to lie with her under the spring sun and have her wild hair tickle my nose, watching her head rise and fall on my chest as I breathed in the new blooms.

"What can I do to help?"

"I don't know. I need to bring them here as soon as I can. I've got to get Ma some work, and Maggie set with school for the fall. She'll have to start back with the younger children."

"If she's as bright as you, she'll catch up in no time. Besides, I can help her. I—" She stopped herself, knowing she wouldn't be here in the fall. She wouldn't be here past the first few weeks of summer.

"It's okay. We'll be fine. Right now, I need to get to the bank and buy some tickets. Wire Dublin in hopes they can leave soon, and call over to Martin to see about a job for

Ma."

"Let me come into town with you. I'll send the telegram. You tell me what to say."

It was a small task that would hardly take my time, but it was a help for Caitrin to be a help to me. Accepting her help didn't disturb me as it typically would have. "Thank you. I could use your company."

"I'll go get my things and be right back." She sprang up and was gone.

***

CATHY

A ride into town with Thomas usually meant we stopped at his land and made love, or at the very least pulled over to a secluded spot to steal some time for kisses and whispered promises we knew we wouldn't, couldn't, keep.

This time, Thomas kept his hands on the wheel instead of reaching over his body with his left hand to touch my knee. His jaw ground together and his eyes fixed on the road, but I suspected he wasn't as attentive to his driving as he seemed.

"I don't think your mother meant to hurt you."

He barked a bitter laugh. "She didn't intend to ruin my plans, but she did." He took a deep breath and loosened his fingers. He flexed his right hand, which I knew seized up at times now that he didn't hide the pain from me. "If only she had said something when Maggie first left school. I could have…I don't know what I could have done."

"We'll figure something out." I rested my hand on his shoulder and he chanced a look at me. I smiled in what I hoped was a comforting way. Honestly, I didn't see a good solution either. Spending all his money to bring his family here and support them meant construction would have to wait even longer.

"Can I ask my father to invest in your inn?"

"No. I won't take money from your father. I don't want him to suspect there is anything between us. And if he did, the last thing I would do is take his money after—after. You know."

"You're impossible. You act like it's the rape of Helen. I'm a grown woman and it's 1949."

"So, how will you introduce me to your parents when they arrive at the opening?"

"I hadn't thought about it." I had thought about it. I had dreamed that we would all eat together. Daddy would laugh at Thomas's jokes. Mother would dance with him and be taken with his charm. Beth would appreciate his humble beginnings. "I'd fight for us, if there was an 'us' to fight for. I'm not taking my mother's path. You of all people should understand that. You're making sure you don't follow your father's fate."

"You've got me there. With Ma and Maggie returning, I won't have much of a home life to offer anyway."

I was going to argue that, but I selfishly didn't want him to offer a home life to any other girl. Yet I knew he couldn't carry on an affair with me forever. He would eventually want a wife and children, not infrequent trips to my future apartment in New York.

He pulled up to the Western Union office. "I'll write

out what you should send. And then I'll go over to the bank while you're inside. Okay?"

"Of course." I waited while he wrote out the message, carefully considering how to keep it as short as possible.

"It's going to turn out just fine. I have faith in you." I pulled him into me and didn't care if passersby could see. He needed a kiss and I wanted one as well. It was a strong one. He needed to know I was there to support him in any way I could.

"Caitrin," he said as we leaned our foreheads together. "I love you."

The seat seemed to give way and my stomach pitched "Don't say that."

"It's the truth. I know you love me."

A sob wracked my chest simultaneous as my heart leapt. "I do love you. I uselessly love you."

"It's not useless. What would I do without you?"

I smiled through my tears. "Have a much easier, but certainly less interesting, life."

He laughed and kissed the top of my head. "That, my love, is true."

We went our separate ways in town. He dashed about to the bank and to the travel agent's. Being in love was the most wonderful pain. Falling for Thomas was worth it. I could carry this love with me in my life, keep it safe in my heart, and know that no other man would ever measure up.

After I sent the telegram, I completed a few errands for myself and Ethel Nussbaum, taking advantage of being in town. And I stopped in the menswear store.

I watched Thomas cross the street back to the truck, his long legs striding with confidence, his flame-red hair shining in the spring sun. "What have you got there?" He pointed to the package.

"I bought you a suit." I held it out. "It might need altering, but I think I know your size. Happy birthday."

I extended my arms, which held the paper-wrapped gabardine suit.

"My birthday isn't until August."

"You need this now. And besides, who knows where I'll be then?"

He swiped at his already reddened eyes but took the package. Carefully undoing the tie, he let the paper fall open and his mouth dropped.

He caressed the fine fabric. "I don't know what to say. I can buy my own suits, you know."

"That's not the point. I want to give this to you. As a memento of our summer. You'll think of me when you wear it?"

He nodded. "It's difficult for me to accept gifts." He folded the paper back in place.

"Don't be so stubborn now. Not when I'm about to abandon you after opening."

"No, you're not abandoning me." His chest swelled with a breath. The familiar determination returned to his stance. "Thank you. It's a wonderful gift. You'll have to wait for a more private place for me to properly thank you."

"I can be patient. For a little while."

"Can you be patient for a bit longer? Since we're

halfway to Glagorm I could stop and talk to Martin about a position for Ma and maybe Maggie."

"Of course, I'd love to finally meet them."

He nodded and we climbed in.

His anger had clearly lessened but tension still pulsed in his temples.

"Penny for your thoughts."

He tried to smile. "It's only…I haven't told Martin and Mary about you. I didn't think that would be right."

My face flamed, and I stifled the tremor in my voice. "I don't expect to be introduced as anyone other than your bookkeeper." I pasted on a smile, not that he took his eyes off the road.

He was right. We had to maintain the distance we practiced at the Belvedere everywhere we went. The Catskills weren't big enough to keep the gossip down.

I had never been over to the north side of the mountains. The landscape was really the same, but I never tired of it. Winding roads led to unexpected views of valley and lakes. Farms were cut out from between thick woods. The air was clean and the constant chorus of birds and insects played in the background.

Thomas pulled the car off the road and down a dirt path at a carefully painted sign announcing the approach of "Glagorm Family Resort." What I had learned to recognize as the St Brigid cross adorned the front entrance.

The main building had at one time been a large farmhouse, with obvious additions and improvements made over the years. A row of attached bungalows spread out to the side. In the distance, I spotted the pond with a diving platform and some playing fields. Horses lazily munched hay in a paddock.

"They're good horses for riding. Some of the city people have never been on a horse. But these couldn't be bothered to get past a trot, let alone throw a nervous first-time rider. And see that pavilion? I designed that; Seamus and I built it."

"It's beautiful." What was even more beautiful was the light in his eyes and the easy smile on his face. Coming here was a good decision. He needed this connection now. "I bet those outdoor lights make it look magical in the evening."

"They do, like fairies. I worked on the wiring. Tricky to bring it out there without making a mess of the front porch." His chest filled out with a satisfied breath.

"Can we say hello to Seamus? I miss him."

"He probably misses you as well, but will never say so. Let's go to my shed. I mean the shed."

His step was lighter as we approached "his shed." I could imagine him working here in a blue work shirt, getting dirty, sweating, and happy.

"Old man?" Thomas called into the darkened workspace. "He's probably off fixing something. I'll introduce you to Martin and Mary." He took my hand to lead me, but remembered our plan and let go with a brief expression of apology.

"You'd better hope they already have a bookkeeper. This place is so beautiful, I'd leave the Belvedere in a minute," I teased.

We entered the main building and before my eyes adjusted from the bright sun, we heard, "Tommy Cullen, what are you doing here? And who is this lovely lass you've brought with you?" The booming voice belonged to a tall fat man with a full head of thick white hair.

"Martin Finnegan, this is Catherine Gold, the bookkeeper at the Belvedere. We had some business in town and I asked if she would accompany me as I have some business with you."

I almost didn't recognize my real name when Thomas used it.

"Business with me? That sounds serious." His broad face broke into an even wider smile than before. "Pleasure to meet you." He held out his hand.

"It's nice to meet you as well. You have a beautiful place here. Your view of the mountain is spectacular."

"Maybe Catherine could visit with Seamus while you and I talk."

The joy in Martin's face dissolved away. "Seamus, the old fool, is laid up in bed. Refuses to see a doctor." He shook his head.

"Is he going to be okay?" I asked because Thomas seemed too stunned to speak.

"Who knows with him. He complains about everything, and has been insisting he's at death's door for the past ten years."

"We'll go see him." Thomas led me to the back of the house, down a corridor, and knocked at the door at the very end.

"Come in, come in. I hear ya boots clomping down the hall."

We entered and Seamus was propped in bed. His hair looked clean for the first time since I'd known him, and instead of his typical work clothes, he wore a clean white shirt. A book rested in his lap opened to a page of poetry.

"You must be sick, I can't remember when I last saw you read a book."

"Ach. I read plenty. Just none of those cheap pulp novels. Miss Gold, I'm sorry you have to see me like this."

"Nonsense. Is there something I can get for you?"

He shook his head. "Mary is waiting on me hand and foot. Just a little stomach problem. I'm already feeling better."

"You don't look too bad." Thomas approached the bed. "You've color in your face and you've even had a bath."

"I know, it's not even Sunday." He moved to sit up and winced. "Only hurts when I move."

"That does it. I'm taking you to the hospital. And before you argue, I'm paying for the bill. Martin can't afford to have you laid up in bed mere weeks from the start of the season."

Seamus began to protest, but Thomas was already at the bureau taking out some clothes.

"I'll wait outside by the truck." I dashed out to give Seamus some privacy as he collected his things.

I passed Martin on the way out.

"How's he doing?"

"He doesn't look too bad, but Thomas is insisting he

get examined. I think we're taking him with us. Maybe they should have checked with you."

Martin shook his head. "I'm glad Thomas came by when he did. He's the only one Seamus will listen to. What was it that Thomas came by for anyway?"

"You'll have to ask him. I think it's a personal matter. I was simply along to take care of some things in town."

"Sure, sure." Martin nodded. His intense gaze unsettled me. "I've got a pretty good view of the front from here." He pointed to where we parked the truck. "Tommy has a lot to offer the right woman. A woman who can understand where he comes from. A woman who won't chase him for his wealth that he's struggled for. A woman who knows how to work hard by his side. He needs a wife who can make shepherd's pie."

"I'm sure he'll find someone who can cook all his favorite meals." I shuffled my feet and wondered how long it could take to get an old man out of bed.

"He'll only find her if he's free to look."

"Thomas is his own man and can make decisions for himself. He's very smart."

"All men can become stupid when they see a pretty face." He raised one eyebrow.

"Thank you for the compliment." I straightened my spine.

"What compliment?" Thomas entered with Seamus leaning on his arm. Seamus looked fit, except for the grimace of pain with each step.

"Martin said I was beautiful enough to make a man

senseless."

Thomas looked between us, but I kept my steely gaze on Martin.

Maybe I couldn't cook shepherd's pie. And maybe I wouldn't fit in with "his people." But I knew what Thomas needed. I knew I could be a help to him at this time.

"We'll call you from the hospital and I'll ask you about that other matter then."

"You know you can rely on us for anything you need, Thomas." Martin wouldn't release my stare. "Your people are always here for you. What's mine is yours. We're *family*."

Thomas probably missed the underlying meaning as he led Seamus to the truck.

"I'll sit in the back," I said as Thomas left. "I know how to put the needs of those I care about above my own as well." This last part only Martin could hear.

Thomas helped Seamus into the passenger seat, and I climbed in back with his overnight bag. Martin had no idea I wasn't after Thomas for his money and land, but was right of course. Thomas did need all of that in a wife. And I could never provide it. I could only keep a kosher home, if I ever kept a home at all. If I ever had a child, I'd have to find someone to care for it. I laughed at the image of my belly huge with a pregnancy waddling into an insurance office to work.

No use in thinking about any of that. Seamus had to be taken care of. Thomas had to finish making arrangements for his family. The Belvedere needed the finishing touches. And I had a few letters to write to set myself up for my own future. With the money I had saved these past few months, I was well positioned to rent a place of my own and get a job that would support me. Daddy couldn't keep me from every company. With my own money to get myself started, nothing stood between me and my future happiness. Nothing except the ability to make shepherd's pie.

***

THOMAS

We needed all hands on deck for the last week's preparations. If I had caught anyone sitting down, I'd likely lash out, calling down every curse I could conjure. But everyone sensed the urgency and I never had the chance to show my temper. In fact, I was mightily impressed with how everyone pitched in. With Seamus safely recovering from his appendectomy, the hard work from everyone was a blessing. Even Ron rolled up his sleeves and helped carry lounge chairs out to the lake. Shelley and Mrs. Nussbaum shelved the books Caitrin had purchased for the library. Caitrin had spent hours deciding on which books to include, making sure there was something for each age group.

She paid no mind to Ron, who insisted that children didn't want to read over the summer, especially when there was a whole outdoors to play in.

The kitchen buzzed with the chaos that was typical to a catering kitchen. But the staff seemed to have already learned each other's places, and they moved dance-like around each other.

Caitrin was in deep conversation with Sam about the lobby furniture. I have no idea how I got stuck with Sam again. I had hoped he would stay at Pine Breeze, but Ron brought him over to be his assistant. I didn't question why the assistant manager needed an assistant. At least I knew what I was getting with Sam.

"We can't have this sofa simply sitting here in the middle, Sam," Caitrin explained. "It's clearly part of the set over there."

Sam looked back and forth between the sofa and the matching chairs. "You want me to move the chairs here?"

Caitrin's eyes grew wide and I predicted smoke would come out of her ears.

"Sam," I interrupted. "Why don't you help with the chairs by the lake? Miss Gold and I will take care of this."

Sam shrugged and meandered away.

"How stupid can he be? Why would we want the furniture in the middle of the floor? I-I-"

I laid my hand on her arm. "You know Sam. He's never going to get it. We'll have to move this behemoth to the sitting area. There isn't an extra pair of hands anywhere."

"Okay, I'm game." Caitrin kicked off her shoes. "I can get a better handle now without those heels."

Her adorable toes were painted and showed through her stockings.

"Stop smiling," she scolded, but her eyes held a flirting look.

I waggled my eyebrows and went to one end of the couch. "On three we lift. One, two, three."

With grunts, we got the sofa in the air. I walked back a few paces and Caitrin was at the other end. The strain showed on her face, her grip wobbled.

"Let's put it down." I laid my side down, and hers came down with a thud.

"Do you think we can push it?" she asked.

"Not without ripping the carpet," I said. "Come on, a few more feet and we'll rest again."

We completed the next phase and she was more prepared and let the sofa down easier that time.

"Phew." She wiped her brow. "I never knew being a bookkeeper would be so physically demanding."

"It takes everyone to make this place run." I fell onto the couch and patted the space next to me.

"Someone will see." She craned her neck.

"Everyone is busy." I beckoned her.

She snuggled into my side. "This couch could easily fit five people."

"I guess that's why Ron bought it." I buried my face in her hair.

She pulled back and patted her head. "You'll muss me."

"I like mussing you." I sighed. "I might not get much time for mussing. My mother and sister arrive in two weeks."

"Oh, so soon?" She lifted her head and smoothed her skirt.

"There was no point in waiting. They cleared up their arrangements in Ireland and were able to get tickets."

"And they'll be at Mr. Finnigan's place?"

"You say his name like he's the devil. He's agreed to take them in and have them work there this summer. He can't keep them all year and certainly can't keep Maggie if she's not working. He has his own mouths to feed. But I can't worry about that now. I'll get them here, and maybe I'll earn enough this summer to keep them in a small place. Ma will have to find work." I stopped myself. I didn't want to ruin one of the last quiet moments we would have together.

"I found a place. I've already paid a deposit and first month's rent. One of the girls from school lives in the building and says it's clean and safe." She laid her head against my shoulder. "I'll have a private place all to myself. Waiting for you to have a free day to come visit me."

"Sounds lovely," I lied. It sounded like torture. Grabbing a day or two a month. A rushed visit after a long train trip. I wanted more of Caitrin, but I couldn't ask it of her. Especially now that I was responsible for two other women. "Does your father know?"

"No, I'll tell him when I get a job. I won't be able to support myself for long without one. No use in confronting him until I'm sure it will work out." She stood. "Let's move this thing."

She hiked up her skirt over her knees. "I can take bigger steps this way."

"But I won't be able to move at all now." I winked.

With a few more starts and stops, we finally positioned the couch where it belonged.

"Almost time for lunch," she said, arranging her skirt properly and slipping her shoes back on her feet.

"I'm not wanting lunch. I'm wanting to see you do that thing with your skirt again. Your pretty lacy slip peeks out when you do." I caressed her cheek.

"Everyone will be coming through here soon."

"That means no one will be in the staff house." I grabbed her hand.

"People will notice we're gone," she hissed.

"Oh, Shelley," I called as we neared the door. "Miss Gold and I have to run into the bank to make sure payroll is ready for all the new staff. Please tell Ron he should oversee the afternoon preparations."

Before she answered, I had led Caitrin to the truck.

"We're not going to the bank, are we?"

"We'll stop there briefly."

The familiar route to my land took no time at all.

"I'm just bursting for opening weekend." Caitin's voice bubbled with giddiness.

"It'll be a feast for everyone's eyes. Mr. Bergen is going to flip."

I pulled the truck over to the side of the road and went around to help Caitrin out.

The path had been worn a bit further from our tracks, but the new growth still made it impossible to hold hands and walk side by side. Emerging onto the clearing, we stopped and looked out over the lake.

"I can barely make out Pine Breeze. Is that the lifeguard chair?" Caitrin squinted.

"Yep. And over there you can see people dragging out those same tired beach loungers."

"Funny how worn they were. I never noticed until we purchased all the new ones for Belvedere. It boggles my mind how much money went into setting it up."

"I don't want your mind boggled or thinking about money." I pulled her back so we were shielded by the trees and kissed her.

She tasted warm and like vanilla. Her soft body molded to mind, and I ran my hand down over her bottom.

She broke the kiss and nearly ripped the buttons on my shirt in her haste.

"We have time," I said.

"I can't wait. I need to feel you." She tugged at my undershirt. Frantically, her hands roamed my back. Her fingers explored every inch, sending hot desire through my veins.

The zipper on her skirt came down easily and I pushed down her slip. She stepped out and flung her sweater over her head. The panties and bra matched, white with tiny pink flowers at the edge.

She worked at my belt but became frustrated. "Get out of this," she demanded.

"Yes, ma'am." I undid my trousers and with just my skivvies, I pulled her down on top of me as we sank into the dewy grass.

"It's chilly," she said, burying her face in my neck.

"This will warm you up." I flipped her over and traced the line from her collarbone down between her breasts and to the edge of her panties. I dipped my finger inside, finding her tight curls damp, and not from the ground.

"Mmmm," she purred and arched her back, her breasts constrained by her bra. "More."

"Just a moment. I need to fix something." I reached

under her and unhooked her bra.

Her sigh could have been from relief. But it could also have been from her beautiful body now bare to the sunlight and gentle breeze.

Taking her rosy nipple in my mouth, rolling my tongue over it, I grew hard. My finger slid up and down her slit. She writhed beneath me. Pleasuring Caitrin clutched my heart, sent my head spinning, and filled me with awe. Her body responded so freely.

"Thomas, I need you," she moaned.

"I need you, love." I choked on the words, because they meant more than needing her for my lusty release.

Shedding my skivvies, I climbed between her legs. She held my shoulders in a fierce embrace. "Take me forever," she whispered.

"Don't ever let go of me," I said as I slid into her.

Her channel pressed around me, the tight slick walls holding me in place. Time could've stopped and I wouldn't have cared. Joining with the most brilliant and brave woman, on the most beautiful spot of land. For one moment, everything was perfect. The worries blown away with the gust of wind.

"Thomas? You stopped."

"Can we stay here forever?"

"We will. We'll always be here together." A tear ran down her cheek even as she rocked her hips, pulling me farther in.

"Sweet Caitrin," I strained the words and I lost control.

I drove into her, and she accepted each thrust, opening

even wider, finally wrapping her legs around my back and riding along with me.

Her orgasm rippled through her and her sex tugged at me. That was all it took to send me over the edge. Shattered, I barely kept myself propped on my forearms. I rested my head on her chest.

"I love you," I said, fearful to move and break the spell of peace we were under.

"I love you." She stroked my hair. "I always will. No matter what happens. You have my heart."

A moment later, we untwined our bodies and lay staring through the leaves at the perfect cotton-ball clouds.

"We should get dressed," she said.

"Yes." I raised myself up on my elbows. "I don't want to beg. I don't want to pressure you."

"Then don't," she pleaded. She turned her back and wriggled into her top. "I could be very tempted to give everything up for you. To live here on this tiny space, looking at the lake every day. But then what?"

"You're right, forget it." I stood and pulled up my pants. No use in going over old tracks.

"Don't be angry." She had dressed and wrapped her arms around my waist from behind.

"Angry," I snorted. "What's the use of anger when it won't change a darn thing?" I unclasped her hands and bent to collect my shirts.

"No, we can't change anything." She stepped into her shoes and waited at the path's opening.

Wordlessly, we walked to the truck and I helped her in.

Instead of turning around, I headed into town.

"Would you be willing to stop in at the hospital? Seamus is still recovering from his appendectomy and I need to settle the bill."

"Of course. He's like family to you."

The drive to the hospital didn't take long, but our silence made it drag. Our usual banter and sharing of dreams had no place in our present. Because the future was unfolding as we drove down Main Street.

"Do you want me to wait here?" she asked.

"Seamus likes you. You should come." I went around to her door and helped her down. After visiting the business office and peeling off more money from my billfold, we went up to the floor he was on.

"Are you here to see Mr. McGillins?" the familiar nurse asked.

"Yes, we are," I said. "How is he?"

She pursed her lips. "He has an infection. Not uncommon for after a major surgery. I'll get the doctor to come talk to you."

Walking down the row of beds, we found him in the same bed as the last time I visited him, but he looked even paler than before.

"Hey, Seamus," I whispered and took the hard seat next to his bed. Caitrin pulled up another chair.

"Mr. McGillins," she said, louder, and it roused him.

"You two look like you're looking at a corpse. Did I die?" he croaked.

"You're not that lucky. Martin has a pile of work

waiting for you, so you can't." My eyes burned. "They say you have an infection." I cleared my throat; something was stuck in it.

"Humph. I'm sicker than when I came in. You might as well bring me home. This place charges more than your fancy Belvedere."

"And the food's not as good." Caitrin placed her hand on his ashen one lost on the field of the starched white sheet.

"Don't worry about the money. I've paid your bill. You can't go home until the doctor says so. But you'd better be well by the time Ma and Maggie get here."

"I do look forward to seeing them. They belong here, your family." He squeezed Caitrin's hand. "I'm feeling right sleepy. Sorry I'm not better company."

"We'll let you rest." Caitrin stood.

I rested my hand on his shoulder. "*Beidh biseach ort go luath.*"

Wordlessly, we walked to the truck and rode back to the Belvedere.

"He'll be okay," Caitrin said.

"Maybe. And maybe he'll finally die like he's been promising to do." I stopped the truck about a quarter mile away from the Belvedere. The deserted road wasn't going to get any use for another week. "I'm going out of my mind. I love you fiercely, but I can't have you. I want to build my inn, but my family, both here and in Ireland, need my money. All the things I want are simple things any man should have. Why don't I deserve them?"

"You more than deserve them." She pulled me to her and our embrace was hard, uncomfortable, and urgent. "Life is unfair. Is there any reason I shouldn't have the job I want? Why should I have to hide my plans from my family? Why should I have to choose between having a family and allowing my mind to work on what I want? The only reason is that the world is unfair."

I wept into her hair. I didn't care how weak it made me seem. I wept for Seamus, and my mother. My father's death and Maggie's lost years not in school. And for the woman who was giving up one future for another. She could've stayed in the Catskills with me. But I didn't dare ask her. I felt her sobs shake her body against mine.

"We're some fine pair." I pulled back and tucked her wild hair behind her ears.

"Some fine pair," she repeated and wiped my shirt front.

"Ready to go back? I bet there's more furniture that needs lifting."

"Let's make this the best resort the Catskills has ever seen." She squared her shoulders.

"It will be," I assured her as I pulled the car back onto the road. I might be losing my girl. I might be losing my dear friend. And I might be taking on a huge burden financially when my family returned. But I had my reputation. I had my job. These things would keep me grounded. I could always rely on those.

Chapter 15

CATHY

I laid my hand on my belly to steady the jumping frogs inside. I stood just inside the reception hall as the van pulled up with the first guests of the Belvedere's grand opening.

"Relax. Everything will be perfect." Thomas's voice was at my ear. He had come up behind me and I felt his presence even though he was too far away to touch. A respectable distance.

"How can you be so calm?" I shifted my feet.

"Because worrying won't make the pool warm enough. Worrying won't get that lunch on the tables any faster. And worrying certainly won't get that lazy Ronald to do his rounds."

"So how will any of those things get done?"

"With persistence, hard work, and the grace of God."

I watched Mr. Bergen personally greet the first guests and direct them toward us. "I doubt God cares much about the Belvedere's success."

"No, he has bigger problems to deal with. But I don't think he'll abandon us in our time of need," Thomas said with a dramatic flair.

He stepped forward as the guests came in and I walked to the side. The bookkeeper wasn't expected to shake hands with the VIPs. But I knew Mom and Daddy were arriving today and I wanted to see their expressions when they looked at the magnificent building. I wanted to personally escort them to the Sutherland Cottage with the Old English theme.

"Well, Cathy." Mr. Bergen had come inside and waited for the next round of guests. "I am impressed. You were quite a team, you and Thomas and Ron. I can safely say that I put my trust in the right place. I'm proud of you all. I don't take credit for all of this myself. I know how much work goes into it."

"Thank you, Mr. Bergen. I enjoyed my work here quite a bit. It will be sad to say good-bye."

"I can't in good conscience keep you here any longer." He beamed. "Your parents will want you home. You've got to go start a life of your own." He dropped his voice. "And maybe find a nice boy to start a family of your own."

I felt myself blush. "I do think I'm ready for the next step in my life." It didn't involve my parents' house, nice boys, or babies. But the letter from Will Hartman was tucked inside my skirt pocket.

I hadn't yet shared the news with Thomas that I'd gotten a job with the insurance company. Actuary. I had a title and everything. I knew he'd be happy for me. I'd have my own apartment in New York. He could come down after the summer and we'd spend cozy nights eating a dinner I cooked at a tiny table in my tiny apartment. It would almost be like we were married.

I took a deep breath and stepped onto the veranda as

the van pulled up a second time.

My parents emerged, and my waiting paid off. I don't think I've ever seen my father's mouth fall open. He was not an easy man to impress. His eyes traveled over the lines of the building and then scanned the grounds.

Mom spotted me right away. She nearly flew up the steps and grabbed me in a hug that made me recall the times when she would cradle me after a fall. The times she held me after my best friend in fourth grade moved away. The kind of mother-hug that magically makes some of the pain go away.

Yet this time, it brought new pain. I realized how I had been separated from her, my family, what I had known and thought was my life.

Somehow, new things, still somewhat unfamiliar, made up my new home. In that hug, I discovered that I could never be her daughter again, not in the same way.

"Let the girl breathe." Daddy put his arms around me too. Which made me miss them even more. Despite my father's overbearing nature, his love for me was never in question. Now I could accept that love freely, because I wouldn't be following his rules as I accepted it.

"You look thin," Mom said with tears in her eyes as she pulled back.

"And if I had gained weight, you'd tell me to watch my figure." I slipped my arm through hers. "Can I be the one to give you the grand tour?"

"We wouldn't want anyone else to do it." Daddy took my other arm.

They exchanged pleasantries with Mr. Bergen. I looked around for Thomas, but he was nowhere to be seen. Although I was sure there were so many details for him to tend to. There would be another opportunity for him to greet Mother and Daddy.

"Simon, can you take this luggage to the Sutherland Cottage? I'm going to show my parents around first."

Simon, the most promising bellboy and waiter we had, nodded and deftly handled my parents' luggage onto a cart.

"My, my. Aren't we the boss?" Daddy said. "I'm so proud of you." He kissed the top of my head.

"Daddy." I rolled my eyes. "What do you want to see first?"

I took them through the main dining room, the solarium, the game room, the library, the ballroom, and the theater. Pointing out all the features and modern conveniences. After seeing the pool, athletic facility, and the beach, we walked by the cottages.

"I can't show you any of the others because we're booked solid for the opening week. Booked for the entire summer, really. But each one is so gorgeous. Ron mostly worked with the decorator. It's amazing what they were able to acquire."

"I can't stop gaping," Mom said. "I'm sure I look foolish, like some country bumpkin."

"You look beautiful and amazed," Daddy said. "And proud. Did I tell you how proud we are of you?"

"Thanks, Daddy." I kissed his cheek. "Here's the Sutherland. I stayed in this one before it was all fitted out."

I opened the door for them and handed Mom the key. There was nothing familiar about the cottage now. It should have felt like a second home given what the structure and I went through together.

The draft from the curtainless windows. The splinters from the unfinished floors. The time a bird flew in through the chimney because I couldn't work the flue. And of course, the evening with Thomas on the mattress in the corner. The corner now adorned with a settee and delicate end table. A plush area rug and rich wallpaper.

"Well, if it was good enough for our bookkeeper daughter, it's good enough for us." Daddy's smile nearly split his face.

"Simon placed your luggage in the master bedroom," I said, pointing down the hall. "I'll let you freshen up. Can you find your way back for dinner? We'll all eat together."

Mom hugged me again. "I've missed you. But I can see all your hard work has meant something."

"I've miss you both, too. Even Beth sometimes."

We laughed and agreed to meet for dinner. I turned as I walked out the door and Mom and Daddy embraced, him smoothing her hair and whispering in her ear.

They may not have the life I wanted, but their love for each other was strong. Plenty of marriages were obviously strained or distant. But my parents were always warm, with each other and with us.

I only hoped Daddy and Mom would continue to be proud of me after I dropped the bomb that was my big news. I could explain that I would meet them every week for

Sabbath dinner. I would live close enough to see them twice a week if they wanted. I wouldn't have to rely on them for money. If I could paint the picture of how this new job would be better for them, their expressions of joy might not wither with my announcement.

Of course, this new job was permanent, not a temporary "lark."

As I neared the office, angry voices shot through the door. The indistinguishable words interrupted each other. I wouldn't have normally knocked before entering my own office, but I did.

After a pause, Mr. Bergen called, "Come in."

When I entered, three beet-red faces turned toward me. Mr. Bergen, Thomas, and a woman I had never met filled the space.

"Hello." I didn't move pass the threshold.

Mr. Bergen straightened his tie and smiled. "Ah, Cathy, have you met Miss Helpern, the decorator?"

"No, I don't think we have." I stepped forward and extended my hand.

"Nice to meet you, again," she said. "I believe I did some work for your mother, that gorgeous addition to your home on Long Island."

"Oh, that's right." I did recall the tall, thin woman, whose silver hair flowed in waves down her back. She wore one of the tunics with bold patterns that I remembered.

"We were settling up our account," Mr. Bergen grumbled while he stared at Thomas.

"I can look for the payments, if you'd like," I said,

reaching for the correct drawer of the filing cabinet. "I've kept all those notes in here."

"What notes?" she asked.

"All the notes you gave Ron." I rummaged through the drawer. "They should be here."

"I gave the younger Mr. Bergen typed invoices, as any professional would do." She sniffed.

"Why don't you look later, Miss Gold?" Thomas didn't take his eyes off Mr. Bergen.

"Well, I'll be going. I can see we'll have to finish this discussion when you have found the invoices." Miss Helpern swept from the room, trailing a heady scent of spicy perfume after her.

Mr. Bergen turned toward me and pasted on his resort owner smile. "Are your parents settled in?"

"Yes, they're meeting us for dinner."

"Excellent. I'm going to meet the guests coming in on the later afternoon train, and then I think we'll have all the chickens in the coop. Isn't that right, Thomas?"

"Yes, sir. Registration and luggage delivery have gone smoothly. I think Mrs. Nussbaum has made some cakes and tea available for people to tide themselves over before dinner."

"Every detail in order as usual. See you at dinner, Cathy." Mr. Bergen nodded and left the room.

With Shelley at the reception desk, and Ronald God knows where, this could be the time to tell Thomas about my job. But something held me back.

"What was that about?" I moved into the room.

"Just opening day complications." His face relaxed and his smile was warm. I wanted to know more, but he probably wasn't going to tell me or he would have by now, and I had other things to talk about.

"It's exciting. I had no idea it would be this wonderful. I feel like we've climbed a mountain and we can rest, admiring the view."

"Let's not rest for too long, or we're liable to roll back down." Thomas shut the office door and pulled me to him. "Hmmmm. It's been days since we've had a visit to my property."

"Nine. Nine days. I've missed you."

"Ahh. The summer is here, your work is ending. It might be best if you return with your parents at the end of the week."

"Are you trying to get rid of me?" I teased. But also wondered why he would want me gone sooner than planned.

"The work becomes dull now." He nuzzled my neck. "And my job becomes even busier."

"I want to tell you something." My breath became shallow as he placed kisses along my collarbone. "Thomas, I can't talk when you do that." I panted.

"I don't want your mouth talking now." He kissed me with a fierce need, a desire and urgency that let me know he wanted to dispel some demon. Maybe the specter of my leaving. The climax of all our work together, which meant its end.

"Oh, Thomas." I fell into his chest.

"I'm going to miss you something terribly, and I've

been thinking it's best if you leave sooner, rather than prolonging our good-bye." His words were rushed, not his typical easy manner.

"But—"

"Besides, we have a regular bookkeeper starting soon. And we're unlikely to find any private time."

Hot tears stung my eyes and I didn't care if I ruined his shirt. "Do you really think that it's best for me to leave now?"

"No. It would be best if I could make the earth stop spinning and we could have this past year forever."

A sob caught in my throat. I pulled back and took out my letter from Will.

"I wanted to show you this." I handed it to him.

"Another man is writing you letters?" His left eyebrow raised up.

"It's only Will Hartman. Read it."

I waited while he scanned the page. "Does this mean you have the career you wanted?" His eyes turned a lighter blue.

"Yes." I nodded, wanting to make sure he could be happy for me.

My feet left the floor as he spun me around. "Oh, sweet Caitrin. I've been sulking, envisioning you wasting away at your parents' home. This makes it so much easier to give you up. They hired you without an interview?"

I ducked my head. "I used the phone to talk to them. I hope that's okay."

"We will never notice the charges. This means you

really do need to leave with your parents. Start your new job. Go ahead and call them. Tell them you'll be there next week."

"Slow your horses," I held out my hands. "I have to buy office clothes, make arrangements to move my belongings from home. I can't just run off right away. Why are you so desperate to be rid of me?"

"I'm simply happy for you." He kissed me again. "You need to freshen your face before you see your parents."

I nodded. "Will you come visit me in New York? There's no one to tell us what to do or how to live. I've saved almost every penny from this job. I'll have a good income. When the summer is over, and you have time. Will you?"

Thomas's face fell. "If I can manage it, I will. If it's in the heavens for us, I'll be there."

I left his cryptic words unchallenged. Nothing could prevent him from seeing me once I was free and independent. But with opening day and my parents waiting for me, I would unravel that mystery later.

***

THOMAS

The ache in my chest was not from eating a roast beef sandwich in the less than two minutes I had in between the day's chaos. The ache bloomed from watching Caitrin walk to her room to prepare for dinner with her parents and praying that she would be spared what I suspected was around the corner.

"Hello, Thomas. Everything seems to be going

according to plan." Ronald Bergen appeared from around the corner of the outer office.

"Hello, Ron. Have you been making the rounds? Are tonight's performers comfortable in their rooms?"

He cocked his head to the side. "I suppose they must be, because no one has said otherwise. Have you seen my father?"

"I had quite an interesting conversation with Mr. Bergen and Miss Helpern. Seems like there is some confusion with the payments to the decorator. I can't imagine what, since Miss Gold is meticulous in her work."

He shrugged.

"Miss Helpern showed up demanding we pay her what we owe her. Said her *invoices* made it clear. Invoices we never saw. Mr. Bergen's investors are here for opening week. It would be a shame if they found out that the place is already in the red."

Ron's eyes went wide.

"Didn't expect to have to make your move so soon, eh?" I said.

"What are you talking about?" Ron's face grew pale and beads of sweat sprung on his brow.

"All those notes you gave me, the ones from the designer, the ones Miss Gold can't find. I should have known. I shouldn't have taken my eye off you."

"You had your eye on someone else," he grunted.

"Leave Miss Gold out of this. This is about the invoices from the decorator. Or should I say lack of invoices. I believed you when you gave me those notes, and I bought your story about how this swanky decorator was too important to be bothered with proper business invoices. What did you do with them?"

"I don't know what you're talking about." The high-pitched tone gave him away.

"I don't know where this is leading, but Miss Gold better not be implicated in this. Her father's a major investor; he'll be terribly displeased if he found out she was manipulated into deceit. I swear by any God you choose I will not allow you to drag her through your schemes and ruin her reputation."

His eyes grew cold, and for the first time in all the years I had known Ron Bergen, he spoke with authority and confidence. "You have no right being worried about her. She is too good for you and if anyone has ruined her, it's you." He poked me in the chest.

If it had been five years prior, I wouldn't have hesitated to break his pudgy finger and knock his arse to the ground. But the wisdom I had gained taught me that it was better for Caitrin if I were around to rescue her.

Besides, his words were true. I had ruined her in the most profound way. That secret would be way more damaging to her than any bookkeeping fraud.

"Do your rounds." I kept my voice steady despite my thundering heart.

I stalked outside to the deserted beach. The guests walked along the path from the cottages to the dining room wearing their best duds. I'd have little time to change into my tux, but if I didn't cool my head, I'd rip my bowtie in two. I wound my way to the shed, hoping to find a moment of solitude.

"Hello, Harold," I said to our new engineer sweeping some sawdust. "I thought you would have gone home."

"Good evening, Mr. Cullen. I wanted to make sure the lifeguard chairs were free of splinters."

"That's very conscientious of you." I nodded.

"Were you looking for me?" His eyes anxious. "I won't show myself to the guests when I leave. I know how to duck around the cottages and make it to the road unseen."

"I know that path too," I said, recalling how Caitrin and I had used it. "But please don't trouble yourself. If you could serve Uncle Sam as an engineer in Europe, you're more than good enough to work here. If anyone says otherwise, you come straight to me."

"I appreciate that, sir." He nodded. "It's not easy finding work. I try not to complain considering what we saw over there. But I at least thought I'd come home to a job."

"My father always said, 'There's nothing so bad that it couldn't be worse.' But he died leaving us drowning in debt. So don't take much stock in what he says."

He laughed and that was enough to ease some of my tension.

"I hope you're happy here, Harold. And go home soon, or your wife will let you know all about it."

We bid each other good night, and I walked with a little more ease to my rooms. Changing into my tux, I took the time to strategize. No doubt, Ronald had done something funny with money meant for the decorator. Miss Helpern had strode in demanding her invoices be paid. After insisting that we had never received invoices, only handwritten notes, she scoffed at the idea she would be so sloppy. When Bergen got into the discussion, he must have seen the writing on the wall. He knew Ron was in charge of working with her.

I should have overseen that more closely. Any fallout from it would ultimately be my burden. I had to make sure to shield Caitrin.

Once she told me about her job offer, I knew I had to do whatever I could to ensure she was protected from whatever was to come.

I might bear the brunt of whatever mistake had been made. But Mr. Bergen knew me. He knew his son. Any consequence would be temporary. He couldn't possibly blame me for whatever the shortfall was.

My tux went on with a little dusting as it had been in storage for the year. Hopefully the scent of mothballs had dissipated.

An air of elation and expectation swirled around the lobby. Crisply dressed waiters directed diners to their tables, and flourished menus. The small set of musicians played quiet appetite-inducing music. Chattering guests wore jewels, hair tonic, and smiles.

I spotted Mr. Bergen seated with the Gold family and approached them.

"Thomas, this is splendid." Mrs. Gold's doe eyes stayed youthful despite her age, and I envisioned her daughters would age as gracefully.

"Thank you, Mrs. Gold. What do you say, sir?"

"I say a toast to you and your staff." He raised his champagne coupe. But his usual easy manner was missing. Our heated conversation with the decorator was left unresolved.

"Here, here." Mr. Gold and the rest raised their glasses as well.

I had avoided looking at Caitrin. She wore a dark blue dress with polka dots, cinched at her slender waist. Her creamy skin displayed by the low neckline, and her ear peeked out from her tamed curls. I knew exactly how to make her moan by kissing right behind her ear.

"Sorry I'm late." Ron arrived and sat at the table next to his mother.

"We were just toasting Thomas's success." Mr. Bergen narrowed his eyes at his son, searching for answers.

"Oh, yes. He did a nice job."

Caitrin sat up in her seat and was going to come to my rescue when she caught the warning in my eye. "Mr. Cullen, why don't you join us?"

The awkward silence sat on us like a damp woolen blanket. Caitrin and Ron were technically my underlings. Yet, they had seats at the table with the gilded-edged china and cut-crystal glasses. I would swallow another cold sandwich in the rushed and crowded kitchen.

"Alas, your company is pleasurable. I have many things to attend to tonight. I hope you enjoy your meal. And make sure to join everyone in the theater. We have singers and dancers fresh from Broadway tonight." I bowed and made my gait as elegant as possible instead of giving in to the storm raging through me.

Only time would tell what would befall me. But more and more I could foresee where the battle lines would be drawn. And it looked like I was odd man out.

Chapter 16

CATHY

"Are you comfortable? Do you need anything?" I asked as we entered my parents' cottage.

"Stop fussing. What more could we possibly need?" Mom brought me close to her and we sat on the couch.

"Cathy." Daddy took the easy chair opposite us and leaned forward. With his fingers laced and resting on his knees, he looked more like he was about to have a business meeting than a quiet reunion conversation.

His business would have to wait. Echoes of last year's fiasco when I blurted out my news rang in my head. This time, there was no doubt in my mind of the outcome. Nothing Daddy could do would change the plans set in motion.

"I need to talk to you both." I took a deep breath. "I know you're against me getting a job and living on my own. But I think I've proved myself this year." Daddy started to interrupt but I stood and paced in front of him. "I've saved quite a bit of money this year. I have enough to support myself in a nice apartment. In fact, I have one lined up." I paused.

Mom gripped her knees with white-knuckled hands, but she produced a strained smile while glancing at Daddy.

Daddy's anger didn't surface. In fact, his eyes turned down in sadness. Resignation had taken the place of outrage.

"I also have an actuary job. At Mr. Blum's company. You know him." I paced once more to the end of the room so I could face them both. Mustering my last ounce of courage even as my stomach tightened, I plowed ahead. "There's nothing you can do to stop me. But I'd like your blessing. I know I can support myself and go far in my career. But it would mean so much more to me if I could share my success with you."

My lungs pumped air as if I had run a mile. The fear was real. I could be losing my parents.

"I think it's a fine plan." Mom stood and grabbed me in a hug. "I'm so proud of you," she said into my ear. When she had finished squeezing me, she released her bear hug and said, "As soon as we get back, we'll go into the city and pick out everything you need for your apartment. Won't that be fun?"

I gulped and tears flowed freely down my face. "Yes. I'd love that." I laughed and cried and hugged her again. Risking a glance at Daddy over her shoulder, I saw him swipe at a tear.

"Daddy?" I stepped away from Mom. "I know this is hard. But we're still a family, right? You're proud of me?"

He sniffed and closed his eyes. "It's not that simple, Cathy."

I knelt before him and took his hands. "Daddy, please. Please don't do this."

"At this point it's not about whether you live at home

or in a box. There are problems at the resort. Bergen pulled me aside and I need to go speak with him. Cathy, it's not up to me if you work or live at home. The matter is out of my hands. And it might be out of yours." He stood and I tumbled back.

Grabbing his hat from the rack, he left without turning around much less saying good-bye.

Mom and I didn't move or say anything for a few moments after the cottage door thumped closed.

"Here." Mom offered her hand to help me stand from the floor.

"What was that all about?" I asked, my shaking legs barely taking me to my mother's side on the sofa again.

"I'm not sure." Mom put her arm around my shoulders but kept her gaze on the closed door. "Your father is a good man. He loves you girls very much. He wants what's best, but he doesn't always see the forest for the trees."

"Are you proud of me?"

"I've never been more proud." She pecked my cheek. "I worry about the choice you're making. I know what it means for your future and I don't want you to have any regrets."

"Mom, don't you have regrets?"

"Sometimes I wonder what my life would have been like if I had gone to law school. Had a career." She let go of me and placed her hands in her lap. "I've never regretted having you girls. But you should know…"

She took a deep breath and picked at the hem of her sweater. This is the story I had always wanted to hear, but now that she was going to tell me I was in no rush. Somehow, I knew that whatever secret she was going to share wasn't going to comfort me.

"Daddy and I met while we were in college. It was the annual synagogue dance. I had come to the dance with someone else, Billy Pasternack." She wrinkled her nose in disgust. "He was my roommate's cousin. He got drunk with his friends and they were stumbling around outside while I stood on the edge of the room with no dance partner. Your father rescued me." She broke into a wide smile. "He had come stag and we danced the rest of the night. After that, he came to take me on walks, and he wrote me letters." A pink tinge came up in her cheeks.

"Mom, did Daddy write you love letters?" I elbowed her in the side.

"I'll never share those letters with you. They are safely hidden." She laughed. "That was my junior year. We dated and I was sure he was going to propose. I was like you, top of my class and had my acceptance letter to law school."

"You did?"

She nodded. "Daddy was very excited. Said we'd have a law partnership." She sniffed, never one to let sadness show. "I got pregnant right after graduation. A month before the wedding. Three months before law school."

"Wait." I counted months in my head of Marilyn's birthday and their anniversary. "Yes. I guess I never did the math before."

She barked a bitter laugh. "You? Not bothering with math?" She dabbed her eyes with her handkerchief. "There wasn't much choice then. Daddy was so consumed with trying to earn a few dollars here and there while in school. And I was scrimping every penny raising Marilyn, and then you. He only ever mentioned that law partnership once again." She blew her nose. "He apologized. He said if he could change things there was no one else he would want to be partners with. But we were different kinds of partners then. Partners in raising a family."

"I still can't get over that you were pregnant when you got married."

"I hope you don't. I hope that's the lesson you take away from this." She took my hands in hers. "You can't have both, honey. You can't make one tiny mistake. Because then your options are closed. And don't believe anyone's promises. I'm not saying Daddy tricked me. But men can't understand. They can't understand the stakes for women. No one is going to watch out for you out in the world."

"I can handle myself."

"Can you? Because even though you'll always have a place to come home to, you will really be on your own. Daddy might be angry now, but he's not going to bar you from coming home, even if that's with a baby."

"Mom," I gasped.

"Do you think I'm stupid? Didn't I just tell you what happened to me? Thomas Cullen is a fine man, a good resort manager. I'm sure he'd make a good husband for someone. But I don't think he's offering that, is he?"

"He did," I admitted. "But I turned him down."

"There you have it. You've made your choice." She

stood and looked out the window, trying to spot Daddy on the darkened path. "I thought I would postpone it for a while. I imagined having a career for a few years first. But it didn't work out that way for me. You're choosing that now, and it might get too late. You might find you love working and suddenly wake up and you'll be thirty, with no options anymore."

"I know, Mom. I know what I'm choosing. And I'll be an excellent spinster aunt for Marilyn's kids." I came up behind her and hugged her. "I know what I can't have."

We stared into the field that separated the cottages from the lake.

The life I was choosing would be a precarious one. But it was my choice. And I wouldn't make the same mistake Mom did. I wouldn't let a man, or love, sway me from my path. No matter how blue his eyes were.

***

THOMAS

"But, sir, I explained it before. Miss Gold recorded every slip of paper Ron handed us." I yanked open the drawer Caitrin had earlier. "The stack of notes he gave us were here just yesterday."

"Listen, Cullen." Mr. Bergen's harsh tone brought me to attention. "I know what I saw. I know what Ron showed me. A pile of invoices from that decorator, all for way over budget. Whatever you were paying her was only a fraction of what she was charging. And now she's demanding her money. All of her money, claiming we never gave her a cent."

Caitrin's father and another man stormed into the office. What had felt like close quarters before now stifled the air.

"Bergen," Mr. Gold began. "What's happened to our money? You say this place is booked solid for the season but you've got no return for us? Blum and I sank a small fortune in with you."

"Cullen and I were just talking about the lousy ledgers your daughter kept." He advanced on Gold.

"Gentlemen," Mr. Blum came between them. "We're old friends from way back. Let's sort this out like *lantsmen*."

Bergen and Gold stared each other down for a moment, then backed off.

"He's right," Gold said. "Start from the beginning."

Bergen adjusted his suit coat. "I'd been keeping tabs on the books from the beginning. Cathy was doing a fine job. And so I didn't peer over her shoulder. Didn't think I needed to. Ron was giving me regular updates and everything seemed on schedule and in budget."

"It was," I interrupted. With three pairs of eyes on me, I steadied my voice. "Cait—Miss Gold is brilliant. The fastest, most accurate bookkeeper there is. I watched her work every day and I trust her."

"You watched her?" Mr. Gold's face reddened. "This was her desk and that's yours?" He pointed to our desks, which at one time seemed too distant and now seemed too close.

"Yes, sir." I stood firm, crossed my arms and set my jaw. I wouldn't come out and explain my relationship with

Caitrin, but neither would I be ashamed.

"Here's what I can guess happened." Bergen slapped a stack of receipts bearing the decorator's name on the desk. "The decorator was going way above budget. Cathy was so excited for this to be the best resort ever, she underreported what the actual invoices were, and never sent on any money. Maybe she hoped to cover it when the money from the guests starting rolling in."

"Cathy would never do that." Mr. Gold pounded the receipts with his fist.

"She didn't do that," I insisted. "If anything, it was Ron. He was the liaison with the decorator. He was the one buying expensive gifts for Shelley. He was the one who told Miss Gold the amounts to pay out. And he was the one Caitrin gave the money to for him to bring to the decorator." I waved my arms and smacked the file cabinet. I shuffled to get some more room, but bumped into Mr. Blum. "This is ridiculous. Why would you suspect Miss Gold?"

"I wouldn't suspect her, normally," Bergen said. "But Ron's shared some other information with me." He turned toward me.

"Has it all finally come out, Thomas?" Ron stood in the doorway, blocking out any fresh air that might have wafted into the overheated office.

"Ron," I growled. "Tell them before something happens to Caitrin. Don't do this to her. Her employer is here." I pointed to Blum. "Don't ruin her reputation."

He sighed as he leaned against the doorjamb and crossed his ankles. "That's a hoot. You being concerned that someone would ruin her reputation."

"What's he mean?" Mr. Gold's voice thundered and he turned on me.

"Mr. Gold, your daughter is brilliant and honest. She would never do what Mr. Bergen is suggesting. You must know that about her." I couldn't let her job, her future, be ruined by Ron. She worked so hard all year to save for her apartment. The pride in her face when she told me about working for Mr. Blum. The determination that not even her father would stand in her way. Her desperation had become mine.

"The question is, what do you know about her?" Gold inched closer. His hot breath of cigar and coffee filled my nostrils.

"Go ahead, Thomas," Ron's weaselly challenge wouldn't bait me. "No? You're not going to explain? Then I will." He pushed off against the doorjamb and took one step into the room. Filling the only free space. "Thomas has seduced Cathy all year. I can't say when it began. But I warned him. Told him to stay away from her." He turned to his father. "I didn't want to say anything. I couldn't bring myself to even think it at first." He shuddered and displayed acting skills I never thought he had. "Let's not blame poor Cathy, she was hardly thinking straight."

"Listen, Ron." I cocked my fist back, but then forced my arm to relax at my side. "Nothing happened between us."

"Really? That's not what Sam says. He's one of the bellboys and waiters. He's been here since the beginning. He even overheard you two in a storage shed back at Pine Breeze. Should I call him in here?" The fat smirking face told me I couldn't deny my relationship with Caitrin.

"Caitrin—Miss Gold—I…" I gave up. Nothing I could say would make this any better.

"You dirty Mick. You filthy—" Gold launched himself at me, with Bergen in between us.

I allowed him to get in a punch to my jaw. It rang in my head, but I deserved one hit from Caitrin's father. When he reached for my throat, though, I swatted his arm back.

"Stop that," Bergen yelled. He and Blum grabbed Gold and held him in place. "Thomas, get out. We'll sort this through without you here."

"Mr. Bergen, you've got to know." I pointed at his son.

"Just go." His voiced softened and his eyes glazed over as they did when he spoke of his deceased son. I had died to him.

Edging past the crush of men and avoiding Mr. Gold's deadly stare, I slammed into Ron on the way out, knocking him on his ass. If my foot caught a rib of his as I left, that wasn't accidental.

The staff house burst with a full complement of employees. Only the work shed would be empty at this time of night. I marched in a straight line, crushing a flower bed and kicking aside a chair as I went.

The sound of Harold's tinkering issued from the shed before I got there.

I flung open the door, slamming against the wall. "Harold, you shouldn't be here. Go home."

"S-sorry, sir." He shrunk into his work shirt and gathered his jacket and hat.

"No, I'm sorry. I've no right to barge in when you're working. But I need a private place, and you have a family." My lungs wouldn't take in air. Cold sweat dampened my neck, and the over starching of my shirt itched against my skin.

"That's all right. A man's got to let off steam. Anything I can do?" He stood gripping his cap.

"Don't suppose you can do anything about the rich sticking together even when they're wrong." I lined up the wrenches on the table in hopes of creating order in my chaotic mind.

"Haven't had much luck with that yet." He smiled and laid a hand on my arm. "You're a good man, and good men don't always win, but that doesn't mean there's no virtue in being good, just for good's sake."

I snorted. "Not sure I believe that."

He nodded. "I'll give you some quiet."

As soon as I noticed his absence, Mr. Bergen appeared in the doorway.

"Thought I might find you here."

I pounced forward. "Sir. My relationship with Miss Gold has nothing to do with this. You've got to believe that."

He hung his head. "I don't know what to believe. My son wouldn't steal from me. That's really just stealing from himself. And I know how stubborn Cathy is to move out of her house. And how you're saving for your own business."

A flame larger than our bonfires blasted through my body. "You said yourself that Ron was an idiot—"

"Don't you use that language about my only son." His voice reverberated off the walls. "I know he's not the brightest, but he's mine. And he wouldn't steal from me. What am I to think?"

"You said you had faith in me. You stood in my office at Pine Breeze, gave me your confidence. Said we shared a past." My throat scratched with the effort of keeping my voice even.

"And I offered you money to open your own resort and you turned it down. It seems you had your own plan to get my money. I was the fool."

"The only thing you're being foolish about is this." I gripped the edge of the worktable. "I've never asked much of you, sir. But I'm begging you. Please don't believe what Ron says. He is the one who took the money. Don't do what I think you're about to do."

"I've got no choice. There are thousands of dollars owed to the decorator, and thousands missing. I've got my two closest friends ready to drag my name through the mud and ruin any chance this place has."

"Please don't let Caitrin lose her job. Can I ask for that? I need your help in protecting her. Blame me if you want. I'll take the fall for Ronald. But she needs that job with Mr. Blum." Bile rose into my mouth, the sour taste of need and weakness I could endure for no one but her.

"I'll see what I can do. Her father is furious, and with good reason."

"It's not her fault, any of it. But you don't want to believe the truth, so you might as well just tell everyone that I forced her to help me. That I threatened her with telling everyone she had sex with me, and I'd ruin her if she didn't fix the books like I ordered her to. Only please let her keep her job with Blum."

He raised his head and met my glare, but his voice was soft. "You need to pack your things, son."

"Don't you dare call me that." My body shook with rage. I pushed past him but was halted by Caitrin and Mrs. Nussbaum rushing toward me.

"Oh, Thomas." Caitrin flung herself into my arms.

I didn't care who witnessed our embrace. Her soft body melted into mine. I fed off her warmth and scent to calm my brain enough to understand what was happening. But she shook with sobs.

"Caitrin, I'm so sorry. I've ruined everything. It's my fault they won't believe it wasn't you."

She lifted her tear-stained face to me. "What are you talking about?"

"Mr. Cullen, we took a phone call for you when we couldn't find you in the office. It was your friend Martin Finnegan." Mrs. Nussbaum twisted her apron hem around her finger.

"What did he want?"

"Thomas," Caitrin wailed and sank back into my chest.

"It's Seamus, he's passed away." Mrs. Nussbaum cast her eyes down and muttered a prayer.

Soft music from the theater drifted across the field. It

wormed into my ear and yanked my heart. Pain radiated from my chest as I sank to my knees. I gripped Caitrin's legs and sobbed into her polka-dotted dress.

Chapter 17

CATHY

Thomas's sobs broke through the still night, drowning out the classical music from the main building.

"I uh, will speak to you later, Cathy." Mr. Bergen tugged at his collar and fidgeted with his necktie. "You need to see me before going to bed tonight." He strode toward the resort.

I watched him go while stroking Thomas's hair. Something had passed between them. I had been searching for Daddy in the main building, deciding that he couldn't hide from me and my stance. When Mrs. Nussbaum frantically pulled me aside to tell me about the phone call, I abruptly abandoned my search for Daddy and instead we scoured the place for Thomas.

Our first stop in the office proved only useful in finding Daddy and Mr. Blum in deep conversation. I didn't allow myself to be waylaid by them. Hopefully, Mr. Blum would understand when he learned that I had to deliver some bad news.

"Will you be okay here?" Mrs. Nussbaum shifted from foot to foot.

"Yes, I'll see he's taken care of."

She turned and scurried back.

I sank to the ground and wrapped my arms around him. His crying had subsided but he wouldn't look at me.

"He loved you like a son," I said.

"Ha. Seems as though I'm losing all my fathers today." He picked up a loose rock and hurled it into the woods.

"You did all you could." I rested my head on his shoulder, reaching for that comfort that typically came from our contact.

"And I'll not spare a dime in sending him off. He'll have a proper wake and funeral. No matter the cost," he said through clenched teeth.

"Of course you will. May his memory be a blessing."

"Memories might be the only blessings I have left." He stood, leaving me clutching the cool air.

His outline scarcely discernable against the dark trees. But the angry sound of his steps crushing the pine needles let me know where he was.

"This probably isn't the right time, I know. But something is going on with Mr. Bergen."

The laugh that carried to me wasn't the kind chuckle from when we shared a joke. A note of hysteria coupled with a harsh edge poisoned it.

For a few moments he paced, swinging his head and gesturing into the night. Foreign grief and anger had replaced the recognizable warmth and love.

He returned to me and dropped to the ground beside me. "Caitrin." He took my hands. "Ron has been stealing. All that money we gave him to pay the decorator, he's spent it on Shelley, or himself, or whatever. But he never paid the decorator a dime."

"Why would he do that? It doesn't make sense." I snatched my hands back. "Ron has all the money he needs."

"But not all the money he wants. Bergen cut off his precious allowance when he started working here. To top it off, Ron's been keeping the invoices to himself."

"There weren't any invoices. Ron said she was too artistic to be bothered with paper." My muddled mind couldn't suss out the meaning of it all.

"Turns out she can be bothered. And Ron wasn't even reporting half of what she was charging. The Belvedere is in debt, your father and new boss want their money, and most of what's coming in has to go to the New York City designer."

"Ron is only shooting himself in the foot."

"Between you and me, that's what he did to get out of basic training."

"That bastard. That no-good bastard. Fuck him." I clasped my hand over my mouth

"Never thought I'd hear that kind of language from those sweet lips. But you might want to save your curses until you hear it all." He bowed his head. "I tried. I really tried. But Mr. Bergen is determined to put the blame on us. On me really."

"No, that's impossible. He knows what a *schlemiel* Ron is." I shook my head. "Mr. Bergen would never blame you."

"What's his choice? To blame his son? No. It's got to be me. And I'm sorry, but you too."

"Fuck!" The word echoed against the sky, rippling

through the night. "No, no, no." I stood and paced. "Was Mr. Blum there? Oh, and my father was there also. That's what he was talking about. No, no, no." I stomped to the work shed and kicked at the wall. "Ouch. Damn it." I sat back down and rubbed my toe.

Thomas rushed over. "Caitrin, we're going to lose our jobs. They're taking our future away. I'll have no money at all soon. I did everything I could. I begged Bergen to let you off the hook, to say it was only me."

"But it wasn't you. It wasn't me. This is so unfair." I couldn't even cry, anger buzzed in my ears, and none of it could be real. Seamus's death, Ron's betrayal. My dreams were finally coming true; it couldn't all slip away again.

"Stay with me, Caitrin." Thomas sat on his knees in front of me. "I have so little to offer, I know. But we'll figure something out. Marry me. I'm a hard worker and will earn as much as I can for you, and my family. It won't be what you're used to, but we'll be together and free. Be mine for poor or poorer."

"I-I can't. It's not the money. You know I don't care about that. It's not even having to care for your mother and sister. It's that I won't be free." Pulling him close was easy; it brought the tangy scent of his aftershave, the heat of his passion, and the ease of his promise. It was rejecting him that was difficult. "Do you see?"

"Yes, but I want you to feel so desperate you'd give up your dreams for me."

"I'd do that for you, Thomas, if I thought it would do either of us any good. What future is there?"

"None. They stole it from us. They won't let us have our future, together or apart." He leaned forward and lay his head in my lap.

"Let's think about Seamus. Let's pray for him." I ran my fingers through his hair.

"He's in heaven looking down and telling me, 'I told you so.' I didn't listen to you, old man. I should have kept my place."

Thomas's place was in my heart. I would never make room for anyone else. But neither could I shove my dreams out of my heart. We were both destined to only have half lives.

Chapter 18

CATHY

My parents left the Belvedere the next morning. They were in no celebratory mood and didn't see the point in pretending to enjoy the luxuries when they knew they weren't paid for.

Mr. Bergen had delivered my firing the previous night, with uncomfortable shuffling and disappointment that still stung my ears. He'd give me a day to get my things together, then I had to leave. Some words about how I could still find a husband were supposed to comfort me.

Daddy wouldn't speak to me but waited by the van with the luggage as Mom stood on the top step with me.

"He's not angry. He's disappointed. Give him some time to cool off." Mom hugged me. "It will be okay."

"He knows it wasn't me, right?"

"I don't think he knows what to think. Right now, he wants his daughter back, his best friend back, his money back. But he will never stop loving you."

"I'll call and let you know how soon I'll be coming back," I said, giving her one more hug.

Daddy watched Mom walk down the steps. He helped her into the van and threw the luggage in the back. Just as he was about to scoot into the seat, he stopped. He ran up the stairs to where I stood and took me in a tight embrace.

"I love you, *sheyne maidel*." He wept into my hair. "I only want you safe and happy."

"I know, Daddy." I gripped his jacket, longing for that contact.

As abruptly as he rushed to me, he released me and returned to the car. He jumped in and the van swung around and headed for the station.

I stood on the step wondering how it could have only been yesterday that they had arrived.

Mrs. Nussbaum joined me. "I left an empty box on your bed," she said. "I found only one clean enough to pack in."

"That's fine, thank you. I guess I'd better get started. Maybe I can make the late train back tonight. I can't stand another night with everyone staring at me at the staff table."

"They know it's all Ron. No one thinks you or Mr. Cullen would steal anything."

"But they believe about me and Thomas."

"Well, we all suspected before. It's one thing to think it quietly and we could all pretend that it wasn't true…"

I hugged her and walked toward the staff house. Hopefully, this time of day most people would be busy and I'd have some privacy in packing my things.

Into my trunk, I packed my clothes and belongings I had brought with me on that cold fall day. In the past months, I'd acquired knickknacks and memories I couldn't part with. The sample towels from the weavers, the perfectly round stone from Thomas's property, the ticket stub from

South Pacific. I'd keep these things in the box Mrs. Nussbaum gave me and treasure them. I could never take them out to admire; it would only bring pain. Like the love letters from my father to my mother, they would stay hidden, bringing ease to my heart in the knowledge they were stowed in some closet of my spinster apartment.

I lugged the box back to the office, remembering that I had a few items there. Some books and my slide rule.

The sun beat on my face, unusually hot for this early in the season. It made for good business as sunbathers could enjoy the lake to its fullest. I stopped to look out that way, and spotted Aaron Litz running out of the water, chasing some squealing girl. He halted when he saw me, raised a tentative hand in a greeting, but didn't beckon me over.

I swallowed the acid in my throat and marched on into the office. Didn't matter what the others thought of me. I wouldn't be in their world for long. I couldn't be in their world; I didn't belong. Not anymore. Not since I had seen what a free life for a career woman could be like. I hadn't yet found my place, but when I did, I'd surround myself with the Miss Helperns of the world, gray-haired women called Miss but who ran successful businesses, and demanded their money from men.

I avoided eye contact with everyone I passed, hoping to grab my things quickly and skedaddle out of this ostentatious resort, hole up in my room at my parents' house until I could figure out my next move.

There was already someone in the office opening and closing drawers and muttering.

Martin Finnegan stood at Thomas's desk, hands on his hips and scowling.

"Mr. Finnegan, what are you doing here?" I placed my box on my desk and faced him.

"Tommy said he left some letters from his mother here, but I can't find them." He too avoided looking directly at me.

"They're in here." I led him to the file cabinet where I had seen Thomas store some of his personal papers. "Everything in this cabinet is his. You should take all of it and let him sort it out."

"Thank you," he mumbled and unceremoniously shoved the papers into a sack he had brought.

"How is he?"

He barked a laugh. "That's rich, you asking how he is. How do you think he is? He's lost his job, his reputation, and his dear friend. A fine pickle you've put him in."

"Me? This is not my fault. I'm in just as much a pickle."

"Hardly. You headed back to your comfy house? You need to find work to support yourself and your two kin coming over from Europe?" He paused. I felt the blaze of his stare on me. "No, I didn't think so. I can't stand here gabbing with you. We have a wake and a funeral."

"I'd like to come. Pay my respects to Seamus. I cared about him."

"It's best if you stay away. You've done enough damage and no one wants to see your type over the hill now."

I couldn't form words to reply. Numbly watched him throw the sack over his shoulder and walk past me. I leaned into my desk to keep from slipping to the floor. His words hit me like the blast of an air raid siren, clattering my insides.

He was right. I had practically thrown myself at Thomas. I'd convinced him that an affair with me would have no consequences. That I wouldn't demand anything from him. But in the end, it was I who'd caused his downfall.

I hoped that he'd find a situation in which he could at least pursue his dream. He still had his land and if he could raise the money, he'd have his inn and the rest wouldn't matter. At least that's what I told myself. Deep beneath what I was willing to admit was the pain of never being in his arms again.

***

THOMAS

The heat inside the pajama factory must have reached past ninety degrees. Fans blew dust-filled air around as I pushed a trolley heaped with fabric toward the end of the line.

"Cullen." The foreman's shout was barely audible above the constant whirl of the sewing machines. "When you finish there, start sweeping the floor. The cutters have scraps piling up at their feet. They can barely move."

"Yes." I still couldn't bring myself to add "sir" when I answered him. Not because he was a bad man, but because I couldn't accept my new role.

Missing a bunch of fingers didn't look good when applying for jobs. Everyone assumed I couldn't do much. Couldn't be of much use. But all I needed for this job was a strong back. A really strong back. Hefting piles of fabric, sweeping, and packing finished pajamas to head to the stores uptown, that was my day. My day after every other day just like it.

I caught Ma's eye as I wheeled the trolley past where she sat at her sewing machine.

"You doing okay?" I asked.

"Just fine." She smiled up at me. Her face dripping with perspiration, her hair tied back in a net. "I'd forgotten how hot it gets here in the summer. But sitting while I work is good."

I nodded and pushed on. Sitting once in a while might be better than her work of cleaning. But sitting in one spot in a stifling factory was not healthy for anyone. She put on a brave face because she believed she still had to do penance to me. I held no anger toward her any more. But I did feel a swell of rage as I passed Maggie's station.

She wasn't as adept at sewing, so her job was folding. Folding, folding, folding. Over and over again. Mindless folding.

"*Comment ça va?*"

"Oh, Thomas, stop that. I'm in America again. I want to make sure my accent sounds like a proper New Yorker." She also smiled in an effort to ease my heart.

"I want you ready for school in a few months."

"As if they are going to teach me French." She shook her head. "I'll want to catch up on maths first."

"Just math, here, Maggie. Not maths."

She nodded, committing it to memory.

I should have felt grateful I found jobs for all of us at the same place. I should have felt grateful I found jobs for us at all. Many women were out of work with all the men returning. And I had to fib a bit when the owners asked about my work in the Catskills. Martin said he would vouch for me working there for him all these years. I wouldn't have to mention Bergen at all. That part of my history had been erased.

All of that history.

"Cullen," the foreman hollered.

I trotted over, my broom in hand. "I was just about to sweep."

He shook his head. "You've got a visitor. Looks like an important person, maybe your banker." He laughed. "You can take your break now. But sweep when the others are on their break. It will be easier then anyway."

"Okay, thank you, sir," I said through clenched teeth. I rested the broom against the wall and exited the factory floor to the entryway.

Garrett stood in his finest suit, a cigarette moving between his mouth and fingers. He paced and looked about him as if he were going to be nabbed any moment.

"Garrett," I called.

"Jesus." His eyes grew wide. "I didn't recognize you. Thomas." He waved his hand to indicate my clothes.

I shoved my hands in my pockets. "These are the clothes I've always worn. At least before I worked at Pine Breeze. No use pretending that I don't belong in them."

"Sorry. No shame in honest hard work." Garrett slapped my shoulder.

"As if you've ever done an honest day of hard work." I

took my cap off and slapped it against my leg to shake the dust off. "Were you able to find a buyer for the land?"

"I can find someone. But maybe you want to rethink it. Maybe you'll save enough and can move back."

"You're some kind of jokester, you know that?" I stepped away and looked out onto the busy street. Trucks blasted black smoke onto people scurrying across the avenue. Steam swirled up out of the grates. Although the noise from the honking horns and vendor shouts eased my ears after the din of the factory. "I can't show my face there. Even on the Irish side. Everyone thinks I'm a thief."

"Everyone knows I'm a thief and it hasn't stopped me."

"Besides, I can't earn enough taking care of Martin's place to keep Maggie out of work. Here, we can live cheap. Ma and I will make enough starting in the fall. Maggie will go to school, I think."

"It's not right that Ron Bergen gets away with this."

"Since when is anything just? What's his old man going to do? Let his only son take the blame when there's a perfectly good Irishman he can toss aside?"

"He didn't seem to have any problems tossing his other son aside, along with the other soldiers when he cheated Uncle Sam." Garrett came up beside me and we stood shoulder to shoulder, watching the traffic and humanity rush by.

"So he purchased a few gallons of milk and some extra meat here and there. Who didn't get a gallon or two of gasoline when they weren't supposed to?"

"I'm not talking about a few black market deals. I'm

talking about how he cheated the army out of food for the boys fighting overseas."

I took a step back so I could look at him. "What are you saying?"

He sighed. "I may be a thief, but I pride myself on keeping secrets. But after how he treated you…" He shrugged. "Bergen helped the local farmers pool their crops and get army contracts to send food to the troops. You would think he was helping and doing his part. But I know for a fact that he skimmed. The army paid for three hundred pounds of potatoes, they got two-fifty. Like that. Then those skimmed potatoes found their way onto the black market. Bergen made money coming and going."

"He didn't. His son was fighting. The older son. He would have never cheated them."

"I saw it with my own eyes. Saw Ronald grease the trucker's palm to sign off on the weight."

The ringing in my ears grew louder. My view of the Bergens had decreased, but skimping on food for the fighting men sunk my opinion of them even lower. I grabbed my head to try to get a handle on Garrett's words.

"Cullen, break time's over. Get back in here." The foreman's voice sliced through my addled thoughts.

"Okay, okay."

"What was that?" He strode toward me.

"Hey, listen, give the guy a moment. I just brought him some bad news from back home." Garrett stepped between us.

The foreman looked back and forth between me and

Garrett. "As long as you're done sweeping before the girls come back from their break." He thrust his chin at Garrett and slunk back into the factory.

"Did you tell me this to rub salt into my wounds?"

"I'm hoping it will spur you to do something. Try to gain your reputation back. Something so you don't give up on your dream."

"There's no way for me to prove that. There's no way I can even contact Bergen at this point."

"I have all the proof you'll need. And I know someone who can call Bergen. You know her too."

My jaw clenched, my gut churned. There was nothing for me to do but sweep the floors. In that moment, I was the most useless person.

I might have neglected to say good-bye to Garrett as I stalked back into the factory. The empty rows of machines created an eerie quiet. Working double-time, I swept each row and amassed a pile of scraps and threads. The sweat soaked through my blue work shirt. I wouldn't do a darn thing with what Garrett told me. It would only open old wounds and solve nothing. I'd still be the thieving Irishman who wouldn't be allowed to run a business in the mountains. But if she could benefit. If she could show her father that she hadn't done anything wrong. Maybe she could clear her name. Maybe she wouldn't have to waste away in her parents' home. If I did confront Bergen, it would have to be with Caitrin and for Caitrin.

Chapter 19

CATHY

Setting the Shabbat table relieved me from the burden of reading the newspaper. Every day for the past two weeks, I had scanned the Friday evening paper for want ads. As soon as I saw something that would take me far away, I would jump on it. I still had money saved in the bank and I could buy a bus ticket to anywhere.

In California, no one knew me. It was no longer a wild west. The movie studios were building Los Angeles into a real city. A big city with big insurance needs.

The mail had also become an obsession of mine. Since I began asking my former professors to write me letters of recommendation, I had waited and waited for their replies. School would be starting soon and they would get around to their correspondence any day now. I'd be saying good-bye to everyone I knew. It tugged at my heart that I might never see my mother again.

She entered with the two loaves of challah. "The table looks beautiful."

"Thanks, Mom." I straightened the napkins. "You'd be okay here, without me. Wouldn't you?"

She froze as she held the soup tureen. "A mother is always preparing herself to say good-bye to her children."

"No, I mean if I moved. Away." My mouth went dry as I forced myself to keep from shaking.

She wrapped her arms around herself and faced me. Lines etched between her brows. "Where are you going?"

"You know I can't stay here forever. And you know what I want."

She nodded. "I want that for you, too. But I don't want to lose you." A tear ran down her cheek.

I rushed forward and squeezed her. "You'll never lose me. Not if you stick by me. I always want you as my mother."

She sniffed and held on to me. "I'll be here whenever you need. And I'll stick by you. Your father might have his ideas, but I have mine. And not even he can come between us."

That's what I needed to hear. I needed my mother's reassurance that I wouldn't lose her, even if I were far away. We let go of each other and wiped our tears.

"Does Marilyn feel well enough to come?" I asked, straightening a napkin.

"She said as long as she doesn't have to smell fish, she thinks she can make it through a meal." Mom clasped her hands. "I hope it gets easier for her. I was sick as a dog for most of my time with her." She sighed. "A grandbaby." Her distracted wistful look gave me time to dash away, since I heard the mailman drop the letters in the box outside.

Daddy walked up the path as I snatched the mail and flipped through, finding nothing that would help me in my escape.

"Anything good today?"

"Just a letter from Beth." I handed him the stack and turned on my heel.

He followed me inside. "Are you ever going to come around? It's been weeks. Don't you think it's time to look ahead and stop moping about what happened? No one blames you. It was that Cullen's fault."

"Give her time," Mom hissed.

I refused to participate in that conversation. Let him think I was still brooding about the past instead of plotting the future.

"All I'm saying is that it shows Cathy doesn't have a head for business. There's no shame in that. Fine, let's move on. She can find a nice boy and we'll all be happy. Eh? Even more grandchildren." He kissed Mother on the cheek and handed her a bunch of flowers. These were lilies.

Every Friday night, he brought home flowers for the Shabbat table. They looked pretty and I had always been excited to see what he had picked for her that week.

No one would ever bring me flowers on Shabbat. I would never set a table for my family. Unless there was a man who wanted a wife who walked in the door with him moments before sundown. There might be one man out there who could accept that. I almost allowed my heart to dream that.

Marilyn and David arrived soon after, and we didn't delay.

Mother recited the prayers. Thanking the lord for the fruit of the vine and the bread from the earth. But it's more than the simple objects we eat and drink. Bread and wine. Life and joy. You can't have one without the other. Work without love isn't worth it. And love without an outlet for your mind leaves you empty.

The image of standing next to Thomas—raising kids, cooking a meal—didn't seem as scary as going to California. Didn't seem a disappointment as it once had.

Conversation drifted to decorating a nursery and all the items Marilyn needed to buy.

"Is it okay that I bring the cradle to our place?" she asked, looking at Mom, but with trepidation in her voice.

"It's in Cathy's room. She always used it for her dolls." Mom dabbed her eye.

I can barely remember when they took Beth as a baby out of the cradle. I had insisted that it be put in my room for my dolls. It had stayed there ever since. Now in the corner, never touched.

"I hardly need it." I shoved a hunk of bread into my mouth.

The rest of the meal proceeded without any more comments needed from me. I helped Mom clear the dishes. Marilyn put her feet up on the couch.

Washing the Shabbat dishes was a slow job. Each one was carefully dried and tucked away for the next six days. I stood at the sink, envisioning myself on my own in California. Catching my reflection in the darkened window, I realized there would be no Shabbat dinners in California. Only a single dish to wash. But I'd be busy. Helping companies offer insurance to people in uncertain times. At least, I hoped I'd be doing that. As long as no one wanted to know what I had been doing in the year between graduation and now.

When my thoughts did wander to this past year, they always went to Thomas. If there was ever anything I could have done to save his job or his dream, I would have. I'd still give up what I could to help. Not that he'd ever accept help from me.

He was not only too proud, but as bad as I felt about what happened to him, he likely felt even worse about what happened to me. Which only made me want him even more.

His face appeared before me, reflected in the window next to my own face. We did make a funny-looking couple. His red hair and ice blue eyes, my crazy curls and deep brown eyes. Opposites in many ways, but the same in the important ones.

His face popped up again and I dropped the soup bowl into the sink. I screamed.

He was outside.

"Cathy, did you break a dish?"

I stared into the sink. Grandma's Shabbat dishes. The ones passed down, destined for the next generation. Now missing a soup bowl.

"I'm sorry."

"Are you okay? It's only a dish. Don't look so stricken."

"I need some air." Without waiting to hear what anyone said, I fled out the back door. I bumped into a familiar body.

I allowed myself to dissolve into his chest. The comfort of his embrace wiped away all the fear and doubt that weighed on my mind. For that moment, I could let love give the illusion of hope.

"My Caitrin," he whispered and pulled me to the end of the yard where no light shone. "I didn't want to call or write. I didn't know how closely your parents were keeping an eye on you."

"I'm not in prison." I ran my hand along his blue work shirt. Thick and impenetrable. Not like his fine white ones he used to wear. "But I am escaping. I'm so glad you're here."

"I can't stay long. I have to catch the train back to the city."

"Where are you living?" I stared up into his face, barely visible with only a slice of moon above.

"My mother, sister, and I have rooms in the Bowery."

"Oh, Thomas. I wish I could do something." I snuggled in closer, not wanting a wisp of air between us.

"My path is clear. The good news is that Maggie can return to school this fall. Ma and I earn enough at—" He choked on his words.

Imagining Thomas anywhere other than in his beautiful suit in the lobby of the Belvedere squeezed my heart. I wouldn't shame him by asking any more questions.

"I'm headed to California. At least I think I am. As soon as my professors send me letters, I'm applying for jobs out there. No one knows me. My father's reach can't possibly touch me there."

"You'd leave your family for good?" He kissed the top of my head.

"I need to be the person I want to be. Not who they want me to be."

"What if I can fix it for you?"

My heart that dreamed the image of a man who could accept a woman with a career thrummed. I could risk my future if Thomas was there.

"I'd give it all up for you, Thomas. Can't we have a future together?" My own prayer that he might ask for marriage again. That it wasn't too late.

"I can't afford a wife now. Even one willing to be poor." His laugh was bitter

"Don't give up anything for me. It would kill me to see you like every other woman. You're not like anyone else and you shouldn't be stuck in anything typical."

I wasn't surprised. Any chance we had together had vanished. He wouldn't take me now that he felt he couldn't support me. And he respected my dreams too much. I'd have to train my heart to accept this resignation.

"Then what is there to fix?"

"Garrett came to visit me. I have information that would discredit Bergen, and Ron. I could clear your name. Get you to show your father that you are good at your work. Make Bergen apologize and get you a job." He rubbed my arms and I was brought back to lying alongside of him on his land.

"Information?"

"He was a war profiteer. He cheated the army out of food for the troops."

"No, not Mr. Bergen. His son Lawrence was there. He

would never."

Thomas held my shoulders. "He did. Garrett can prove it. We need to meet with him, confront him, and threaten to expose him if he doesn't take back what he said about you."

I shook my head. "It can't be." I leaned into him again. I could feed off his warmth. "I've missed you."

"Sweet Caitrin." He stroked my hair. "I can't afford to even think about you, let alone miss you. I'd get so lost in my sadness, I'd never come out. Let's get your name back. Then my pain will be eased knowing you got what you worked so hard for."

"What about your name?"

"It was never worth that much. Garrett is selling my land." He pulled away and stepped to the end of our yard. Turning his back to me, he looked out into the dark, even though there was nothing for him to see.

"You can't sell it. All your plans."

"We have to eat." His shoulders hunched up. "When can you see Bergen again?"

"I'll probably see him at High Holiday services."

"Will Ron be there?"

"Everyone will be there. It's the start of the New Year. We're supposed to look back and think about all the sins we committed and try to make them right. We pray that we're written in the book of life."

"I should have figured there was a book." He laughed. "I'm going to meet you there."

"Do you think that's a good idea?" I didn't resist the urge to fit into his arms one last time.

"No, but I have the name of the truck driver who watched the whole thing. It will be stronger coming from me. Besides, I don't want you to confront him on your own."

"You can't protect me when I'm in California," I mumbled into his chest.

"You don't need protection. You need a good start in life, and I want to give you that, considering what I took from you."

"You didn't take anything I didn't want to give. Besides, it was me who ruined you. Convinced you that an affair wouldn't harm either of us. It was selfish of me to think that way."

"Not selfish. Wishful."

We stood silently in the darkened yard. The leaves in the trees whispered their warning. This would either clear the path for our futures or be the final destruction. With Thomas's arms around me, I realized I couldn't be afraid for anything that came our way.

***

THOMAS

Wind whistled past the imposing stone building. No windows opened onto the front, but stained glass adorned the cupola. The doors appeared small, dwarfed by the massive set of steps and columns.

I'd never been inside a Jewish synagogue, and today didn't seem like the day to start. Caitrin explained that it was a very important holiday, a High Holiday, and that the sanctuary would be bursting. She also explained that she and her mother and sisters would be sitting apart from her father. Men weren't allowed onto the women's side, so there was no point in me coming in to find her. I'd just cause commotion.

I had a feeling that there would be commotion no matter what.

I checked my watch and was about to abandon the entire plan when I spotted a figure hunched against the wind walking toward me. His coat flapped out, exposing his worn pants.

Closing the space between us, I asked, "Are you Johnson?"

"That's my name. You're Garrett's friend. He said I'd recognize you by your carrot top."

We shook hands.

"Thank you for meeting me here. I hope it doesn't cause trouble for you."

He shrugged. "No trouble for me. I saw what I saw. The police didn't believe me then, can't imagine anyone will believe me now. But Garrett paid my fare here and gave me a little pocket money. This squares my debt to him. Don't ask me what he did for me. Besides, if it means those rats get what's coming, I'm happy to help out."

"You went to the police?"

"'Course I did." He stood up straighter. "I saw Bergen grease the palm of the inspector, saw him take his cut of the goods. Saw a diminished load headed out to the boys in Europe." Johnson shook his head. "My brother was there.

He came home all well and good. But told me stories. They were cold and hungry."

"What did the police say?"

"Bah! They never even wrote down what I had said to them." He blew on his hands and stamped his feet. "Colder than usual for this time of year."

"Yes, sorry for having to wait outside. I don't think we could get close to Bergen anywhere else. We know he's inside and has to come out this way. Shouldn't be much longer."

He nodded toward the building. "What do you think they do in there?"

"Pray, I guess. Probably not so different as a church."

"Hmpf." Johnson didn't seem to agree, but I didn't need him to accept Jewish people, just bring down one in particular.

"The plan is to confront Bergen. Let him know that you can identify him and what you saw. We're just going to threaten him with the law."

"Gonna blackmail him?"

"Something like that." I searched for words to explain my obligation to Caitrin. How she deserved the future she'd created for herself and then how it fell apart. All because of me.

I didn't have time to explain. The doors opened and people spilled out. Chatting and grabbing their best hats so as not to lose them to the wind. Some people stopped to talk in small groups; others hurried away, not wanting to spend more time in the cold.

Johnson and I stood at the bottom of the steps, scanning the crowd. I looked from right to left and back again. I didn't want to miss the one chance I would have. Johnson was unlikely to make another trip in for this; he probably didn't owe Garrett any more favors.

"There they are." Johnson pointed to the door on the left.

Bergen held his wife's arm on one side. Ron was on the other. Carefully, they worked their way through the crowd and down the steps. The Gold family was behind them. Caitrin spotted me and waved.

She wore the same heavy coat she'd worn all winter. A blue hat perched on her head and contrasted with the deep brown of her hair and her pale skin. When our eyes locked, I forced my feet to remain on the pavement. Fighting the urge to run to her, grab her, and take her away where she could be who she wanted. Even if that wasn't with me.

She said something to her parents and tapped Bergen on the shoulder. He raised his face and his stare also made me want to rush forward. Only to sock him in his fat jaw. His grim expression was only outdone by Mr. Gold's. His face turned as red as his wool scarf.

"That's him," Johnson said as the entire party approached.

Mr. Gold stumbled down the last few steps and came within an inch of me. "I'll kill you. So help me God, I'll kill you." He kept his teeth clenched so no one around us took notice of his words.

"Mr. Gold, I have no business with you. We're here to

see Mr. Bergen." I forced civility into my voice and risked looking at Caitrin.

The sadness in her face told me that even though we were doing the right thing, even though she might be able to get her job back, we were destroying a man she had grown up with. A man whom her father had trusted as a brother.

"Maybe we'll walk ahead," Mrs. Gold said, touching her husband's shoulder.

"We're staying right here." Mr. Gold folded his arms.

"Thank you, Gold. But I don't think I need your help with this. Whatever Cullen wants, he won't get. If he's here for a handout, he'll be disappointed."

I waited a beat and the wind took that moment to die down. Clouds parted and the sun blazed, reflecting against the house of worship where all the lessons Gold and Bergen heard seemed to have left their minds. Unless today's sermon was on how to extract revenge and commit violence.

"Go ahead, Thomas." Caitrin came to stand by me. She linked her arm through mine and the jolt of love lifted me. I could do anything with her by my side.

"Cathy," her father warned.

Ron remained silent and slunk to the back of the group.

"Thomas has something to say." She caressed my hand.

"Mr. Bergen, this man here is Johnson. You might recognize him from driving the truck for the farmers' collective you managed during the war."

"Never seen this man," Bergen grumbled.

"He's sure seen you. Cheating Uncle Sam out of the food you sold."

"What nonsense is this? We're leaving." Bergen turned to look for his family.

"No, you need to stay." Caitrin's voice was loud enough to attract the attention of the few stragglers. "You owe me something, don't you? You owe me five minutes."

Bergen didn't answer, but he at least paused and awaited what was next.

"Johnson saw you take pounds of food off the scales. He saw you accept payment for the full order and give the government man a bribe to go along with the plan. Then you sold that food on the black market, pocketing even more money."

"Ha. Rubbish. I've never heard such a tale."

"Me neither." Gold cut in. "This is some kind of desperate attempt to win back my daughter. Come, Cathy. We're leaving." He yanked her away.

"No, hold on, folks," Johnson spoke for the first time. "This isn't the man I saw."

"What?" The pull of Caitrin away from me threw me off balance. But this nearly knocked me down. "You said it was Bergen."

"Not this Bergen. That Bergen." He pointed to the edge of the street where Ron had wandered off to. "He recognizes me. Sure as anything."

Ron kept his head ducked down, examining his wingtips.

"Ron, what's this man talking about?"

"I dunno." Ron twisted, facing the opposite direction.

Johnson, with something to prove, marched over and

spun Ron around. "Sure as anything, this is the guy stealing food from the troops and dealing on the black market. He thought I didn't notice. But I'm no fool. I could see what was happening."

"Ron?" Bergen's voice shook.

"Dad, you're not going to believe this guy, are you?" Ron's face flushed but he managed to maintain some bravado.

"You calling me a liar?" Johnson stepped forward.

I held him back, watching the changing emotions on Bergen's face.

"You did," Bergen said in a whisper. "I could always tell when you were lying."

"Aww shucks, Dad. You bought things on the black market all throughout the war." He kicked at stone.

"I never cheated the troops out of food. That would make you a-a…"

"I think you're looking for the word 'profiteer.' Your son left the boys fighting with less food so he could earn a few extra bucks." It gave me no pleasure to say it, but it had to come to light. If only for Caitrin to have some leverage.

"Ronald." Bergen sounded as if he were being strangled. "Your brother was over there."

"That's all I ever heard about. Lawrence this and Lawrence that." Ron threw up his arms. "How much of a difference could it have made?"

"That's not the point." Bergen broke down and an anguished cry escaped his mouth.

Gold shoved his hands in his pockets. "Are you proud

of yourself, Mr. Cullen? Have you gotten your revenge? Happy now?"

"No, sir. That wasn't my goal today. I'm here to help Caitrin. She deserves to have her named cleared. You all know she did nothing wrong. You need to get her job back. The one at the insurance company. I have plenty of contacts still up in the Catskills. They'll listen to me and Johnson here. Once people get a whiff that the Belvedere was funded by war profiteering, you can watch your guests leave in droves. And I think Mr. Blum will believe me in an instant when I explain that it was really Ron who stole that money from the resort."

"*Cathy* doesn't need a job. She has family that will take care of her."

"Daddy, I do need a job. I hate bringing Ron's theft out in the open. But it's the only way to get you and Mr. Bergen to listen." She stood halfway between me and her father, uncomfortable with the reality of what we had just done.

Mr. Bergen had regained control of himself. "I'll do whatever it takes to get rid of this problem. Mr. Johnson, how much money do you need to stay silent?"

"Don't need money. Just a good word from you with the farmers' collective. I think I can get a permanent job hauling for them."

"Done." Bergen straightened his hat. "Cullen, what's your price?"

"I'm not asking anything for myself. Only for Caitrin. You get her the job back and I'll be gone from your lives forever. I don't even live upstate anymore."

"Fine. Gold?"

"Does it mean you'll never come near my girl again?" Mr. Gold hissed.

"It will be the hardest thing I will ever do. But I'll let her go. I'll let her work the job she wants. Live the life she wants. I won't hold her back. Because seeing her happy will soothe the searing pain in my heart when she's not with me."

"Oh, Thomas." Caitrin fell into my arms, trembling with tears.

"Shh, my love. You'll be fine." I stroked her wild hair one last time. "Let me go so you can move forward."

"Never."

***

CATHY

"Never." I gripped his coat. In that moment, I realized that having a career was important, but not so important that I would have no one to share it with. Being alone wasn't a price I was willing to pay. "I won't give up one dream for the other." I looked into Thomas's eyes, finally finding the answers. "We just sat through hours of teaching and prayer. And I didn't hear one thing about having to choose between a career and a family."

Thomas cocked his head and smiled, but before he could respond, Daddy interrupted him.

"Cathy, let's be realistic."

"I'll tell you what's realistic. If I don't get my job back, I'll find something else. You can't stop me. I have money saved. You're the one who's going to lose me, not Thomas. You may already have."

"Cathy, don't say that. I love you." Daddy stepped forward, then halted when I didn't release Thomas.

"You love the girl you want me to be." I let go of Thomas's coat but stood beside him. "You sent me to school. You impressed upon me how important education is. Well, it worked. I'm sorry you have no sons, but you can at least be proud of the daughters you have."

"I am proud of you. But you have an obligation to your people."

"My people? Who are my people? The ones you tell me I belong to, or the ones I chose to belong to?" I slipped my hand into Thomas's, where it fit naturally.

"Cathy's right." Mom pushed in front of Daddy. "You men need to stop being so blind. Blind to the realities of what our kids need. Bergen, you need to rein in your son. He needs a strong hand and some guidance. As well as the love and attention he is due. Just because you lost one son doesn't mean you need to discard this one."

Mr. Bergen's mouth fell open. Ron's expression mimicked his father's.

"And you." She pointed a finger into Daddy's chest. "Our daughter is in love with this man. He's a good, honest man who works hard. And if it weren't for Ronald, he'd still be working at the Belvedere in a position to provide her with a good life. A life she could even provide for herself if we let her."

"She's going to do that anyway, Mr. Gold." Thomas released my hand. "Believe me, I've tried to keep her for myself. Selfishly, I thought I could have her. But Caitrin belongs to no one." He looked me in the eyes. "Sweet Caitrin."

"Thomas, I'll stay with you. I'll be yours for richer, but more likely poorer." I covered his mouth with my gloved hand to prevent him from objecting. "I don't care if we live in a cramped tenement with your mother and sister. I don't care if we can't afford meat every day. I want to have a family with you. Work with you to build a life where we can be together and no one will judge us."

"Don't give up, just for me." His voice barely audible above the wind.

"For us." I planted a kiss on his lips and did hear Mom's gasp, but didn't care.

"Catherine." Daddy's voice broke in.

"I love him. I'm going to get any kind of work I can, and we'll be together."

"Do you know what you're asking of me?" Daddy's eyes misted.

"She's asking you to love and accept her." Mom slid her arm through his. She kissed his cheek. "I know you already do, if you get past your stubborn ideas."

"Mr. Gold, I will take care of Caitrin as best as I can." Thomas spoke to my father, but his smiling face was turned toward me. "She's made up her mind. And what Caitrin Gold wants, Caitrin Gold gets."

"Don't I know it," Daddy said.

We all turned to face him. "Daddy?"

He shook his head. "I don't need to like it. You don't seem to need my blessing. But…it's the New Year." He straightened his hat. "Bergen, you can vouch for Cullen? You think he's a good man?"

"I've always known he was loyal and quick. I should have trusted my gut instead of ignoring the signs." Mr. Bergen held his face in his hands. "I'm sorry. If I can restore your name, Thomas, I will. And I'll call Blum about your job, Cathy. Ron will have to pay back every cent he owes me and my investors. How do you like washing dishes, Ron?"

Ron squeaked in protest but knew when his fight was over. Mr. Bergen's apology went a long way to soothing the embers of anger in my gut. Deep down, he was a good man who, like all of us, was scarred by the war. Living with the loss and tragedy had made all of us doubt and act from fear.

"I'll make it right with you, Gold," Mr. Bergen continued. "I can't have this be the Rosh Hashanah that I carry sin into the next year. You'll get your money back with interest. I owe you. Might wipe me out for a while, but I want to be square with my friends." He turned to Thomas. "Cullen, do have any good ideas for a new investment opportunity for my friend, Mr. Gold?"

My heart flew at the same time that I gulped tears.

"I have an ideal piece of property, ready to be cleared and built on." Thomas wound his arm around my waist. "Sits on the edge of Liberty Lake."

"I see, and do you have someone who can help get this business up and running? Anyone you think is up to the task?" Bergen's sad smile was the beginning of his atonement.

"There's only one person I would want by my side as I

build my future. If she'll accept the position."

"Just until I find a better offer," I teased.

Thomas swung me around and laughter erupted from both of us. He placed me back down and extended his hand to Daddy.

"Sir, I promise you Caitrin will be happy every day."

"It seems I have to trust Cathy to find her own happiness. I'm making no promises about the investment. You might have my daughter, but at least I still have some say in my bank account." Daddy embraced Mom and she wiped a tear.

"Another wedding," Mom sniffed.

"We've got to be going, but I'll be sure that everyone knows Thomas Cullen's new inn is a nice, simple place for families." The Bergens walked away. Ron trailed behind, muttering about the heat in the kitchens in August.

Daddy hesitated but thrust his hand out to Thomas. "I guess this is welcome to the family. You have a lot to learn if you're going to married to one of the Gold girls."

"Thank you, sir. I have the brightest teacher there is." Thomas's smile stretched across his face. "Caitrin, you're making me the happiest man in the world. There are no limits to what we can do together."

"Only in America," I said.

We kissed with the promise that no matter what we faced, we would face it together. That nothing would stand in our way. That love wins over fear. And that love is the most important dream.

Epilogue

Liberty Lake glistened as the sun rose at its edge. A gust of wind pulled the scarf off my head, causing my hair to come loose and wrap around my face. I tugged it free as giggles came from somewhere around my knees.

"Mammeh, your hair is in your eyes." Four-year-old Rebecca Bridget Cullen jumped up to try to swat my hair.

Smiles came to my face frequently with my bubbly girls around.

"Please, go fetch my scarf." I pointed to where it had landed in a bush at the edge of the picnic area of Twin Deer Inn. My husband's dream come true. "And watch the *boychick*." I nodded to Abraham Seamus Cullen, the two-year-old who insisted on following his sister everywhere.

"*When I first came to this land I was not a wealthy man…*" Thomas's voice carried on the wind.

He and Harold hefted outdoor tables into place, and Harold's wife, Nora, followed with a chair in each hand. Their three children poured out, spotted Abe and Rebecca, and wasted no time in joining in whatever mischief the five of them could create.

"Can I get the rest of the chairs?" I asked, approaching the group.

"*So I got myself a wife and I did what I could…*" Thomas

continued to sing.

"Shouldn't you be getting into town?" Nora asked. "It's almost nine."

"I do need to fix my hair and get ready. The representatives of the farm collective are coming in today." I smoothed my skirt.

"That's my brilliant hardworking wife." Thomas had no qualms about kissing me on the cheek in the middle of all the chaos to get ready for the season.

Since opening my small insurance and investment business catering to family farms, I hadn't been able to help much around the inn.

"I'll try to get back to at least watch the kids," I said.

"*Seanmháthair* Cullen has that well in hand," Thomas's mother called as she stepped outside. She'd slowed down in the past few years. But what her body had lost in vigor, her spirit had gained.

She took a seat in one of the chairs and called the five children over to learn yet another Irish folksong. I hoped it wasn't about drinking or dying in some battle. But the joy in her face made any awkward questions from the kids later worthwhile.

Thomas pulled me to his side as we gazed at the main house, painted white with bright blue trim. For the past three years it held us, Harold's family, and still had three spare rooms to let out. But with more children it strained at the seams. The new bungalows stretched away from the main building and into newly cleared land, which Thomas and Harold were working on to make a tennis court and the baseball diamond Harold insisted was essential.

"This is the year I return your father's investment. The income from those extra rooms will put us over the top." Thomas pointed to the still-wild land opposite the bungalows. "Next year, stables and horses. I want our kids to learn to care for horses."

"Sounds lovely." I kissed him. "And smelly."

He reached to my side to tickle me and I squealed as I backed away. But I allowed him to catch me and give me one more hug before I had to get ready to go in to my office. My office.

"Hmmm. I'm sorry I can't be here more frequently." I still fit nicely in his side, as if his body was made as jigsaw piece for only mine.

"Bah. Maggie is getting out of school in a few weeks, and she'll be earning her keep this summer. I'll have to hire a few more cleaning staff, but we'll make do."

A crash resounded from across the lake. We all turned our heads and watched as a small figure directed men and a large backhoe.

"That's got to be Ron overseeing the renovations to Pine Breeze." I held up my hand to shield the sun and squinted into the distance.

"It's taken him all these years, but he's paid back every dime and seems to have settled into a life for himself."

"Didn't have much of a choice with that rushed wedding to Shelley. He had to earn a living."

"Had them one of those premature babies that weigh eight pounds." Thomas winked. "Even your father and

Bergen seem to be on good terms now. Grandparenthood has softened them all."

"Speaking of my father…that can't be their car already." I craned my neck to see where the engine rumble was coming from.

"They must have started driving last night to get here this early." Thomas squared his shoulders. "We haven't finished the painting yet, or setting up this space." Still feeling he needed to prove himself.

"Relax, Daddy doesn't notice anything beyond his grandchildren anymore." I ran up to the drive to meet them. "Hi." I waved.

Sure enough, I received the briefest of pecks and acknowledgments before they rushed down the hill to find the kids.

"Where are the little *psihers*?" Daddy called.

All five kids crowded him as he handed out the usual candies he brought them.

"They shouldn't eat candy this early in the morning." Thomas's mother stood and placed her hands on her hips.

"A little candy won't hurt." Mom had come up beside her and cradled a Pyrex dish in her arms.

They eyed each other as wrestlers circling just before engaging in a match.

Mom held up her dish. "Now, I brought a brisket. I'll just find some room in the icebox for it." She headed for the kitchen door.

"But I have a beef corning in there." Thomas's mother hurried after.

"Do you think they realize it's the same piece of meat in a different sauce?" Thomas asked.

"Would it matter?" I wrung my hands. "Are you going to be okay with the battling grandmothers while I'm at work?"

"Don't even think about missing your important meeting. Your secretary can't hold back those burly farmers for long. Go along and get yourself all professional and we'll be waiting for you when you get back."

"How did I get so lucky with a husband as wonderful as you?"

"Do you know where we're standing?"

"On our property, Twin Deer Inn, that overlooks Liberty Lake and is booked solid for the season."

"This is the exact spot where the old still house stood. You can see the depression over here." He kicked at the ground.

"Oh." I felt my face warm and I turned away from where Daddy played tag with the kids and Nora and Harold raked up fallen pine needles. "I suppose that newly cleared land needs to be christened."

His wicked grin sent fire through me. "Well, the bungalows aren't fitted out with furniture yet."

"That's never stopped us before."

He tipped his head back and laughed.

Suddenly, my feet left the ground as Thomas spun me in a circle. When I landed, his lips were on mine and our kiss held a promise of a future filled with celebrations, struggles, and family. A large family made up of anyone who would join us at Twin Deer.

"Now, my wife, *meaning to my life*," he sang. "Go and earn your bread and make sure those farmers have their future assured."

"No one can know the future," I said with a wink.

"It doesn't much matter what comes our way." His blue eyes still crinkled at the corners when he smiled. He still held me with the same affection. Our love for each other hadn't changed one bit.

The only thing that had changed was the confidence we found when we found our place in the world.

THE END

ABOUT KATE FOREST

Award-winning author Kate Forest has worked in a psychiatric hospital, as a dating coach, and spent a disastrous summer selling aboveground swimming pools. But it was her over twenty-year career as a social worker that compelled her to write love stories with characters you don't typically get to read about. She lives in Philadelphia with her husband, two kids, and a fierce corgi.

You can find her at:
www.KateForestBooks.com
Twitter: @KateForestBooks
Facebook: KateForestAuthor

INTERIOR DESIGN and OTHER EMOTIONS

There are side effects to falling in love.

Gina Giancarlo is an interior design genius, fast as lightning with numbers…and autistic. Yearning to be just like everyone else, she joins a drug trial that promises to help her experience a full range of emotions.

With the ink still wet on his MBA, Chris Rinaldi has only two goals—make bags of cash and bag lots of women. Dancing on the edge of insider trading, he pushes his company to buy stock in a pharmaceutical firm because of its promising new autism drug.

As Gina's understanding of the world blossoms, she forms a connection with the Wall Street hustler, who appreciates her—quirks and all. And for the first time since his sister's death, Chris experiences true emotions with a woman who has recently discovered passion herself.

Gina believes that the pills are responsible for her awakening. Chris knows they're responsible for his success. When the drug is discontinued, the cost of "normal" might bankrupt their future.

IN TUNE OUT OF SYNC

No one wants to play second fiddle in love.

Veronica "Ronnie" Lukas has one dream: playing violin with the New York Philharmonic. She'll do whatever she can to hide her dyslexia and inability to read music, because nothing, not even sexy and talented Scott Grossman, will stand in her way.

Since he first tucked a violin under his chin, Scott's tics caused by Tourette's Syndrome quieted. His talent has thrust him into the harsh spotlight, becoming a reluctant poster child for living with Tourette's.

When Scott wins first chair of a small regional orchestra, Ronnie begrudgingly accepts second. She wants to hate the humble man who is disarmingly open about his disability. Instead, she falls for his heavenly music—and toe-curling kisses. Despite keeping her dyslexia a secret, Scott is smitten with the brilliant woman who doesn't treat him with kid gloves.

There's only one spot open in the New York Philharmonic, but Scott and Ronnie find it's not the competition but their differing views that come to a crescendo—secrets versus truth, spotlight versus shadows. Finding their rhythm is tough when they're marching to their own beat.

Made in the USA
Middletown, DE
20 March 2019